EBURY PRESS
THE LIVING LEGEND

Vayu Naidu's PhD and postdoctoral methodology was in the epic and oral traditions of the Ramayana and the Mahabharata in India and Western theatre. Vayu Naidu Intercultural Storytelling Theatre was founded to explore storytelling in contemporary complex situations and performance. She is a visiting fellow at the Royal Academy of Dramatic Art, where she teaches Indian theatre, and is a writer of historical fiction and myths. Her plays have been broadcast by the BBC. She is a Royal Literary Fund Fellow and Professor of Practice at SOAS, UK. She and her husband live in London and Mammallapuram. For more on her work, please visit www.vayunaidu.com

ADVANCE PRAISE FOR THE BOOK

'The metaphor and the reality of the forest—as a place of exile, a place of refuge, a test of survival, a trial of strength, a path to transformation—taken from the ageless epic of the Ramayana and its many iterations'—Namita Gokhale, Sahitya Akademi Award-winning writer, and founder and co-director of the Jaipur Literature Festival

'Naidu has excavated compelling reimagining to help us appreciate our troubled times. This is an authoritative, visceral and unforgettable contribution to one of the greatest stories ever imagined. Essential reading'—Daljit Nagra, chair and fellow of the Royal Society of Literature

'Epics are often the heartbeats of culture, particularly those like the Ramayana, which is essentially a human story, and a timeless one. Such classics have universal appeal and everlasting relevance because even though our food, clothes, languages and customs change, our basic nature remains the same. The Ramayana is a story that captures the myriad hues of human nature, the complex contours of its reactions, predicaments and contradictions. It becomes more relatable when the story is decontextualized, its tropes examined through a contemporary lens, which is what Vayu sets out to do yet again, after enchanting her readers with *Sita's Ascent*. I am excited to embark on this journey'—Dr Prema Padmanabhan, ophthalmologist and medical research director, Sankara Nethralaya

'This perceptive account of the *Ramayana Tales* encourages an important appreciation for how our environment shapes our decisions'—Rahul Ramakrishnan, Dulwich College U19 Rowing Cox Team England

'*The Living Legend* is a must-read for anyone who wishes to explore the profound wisdom of ancient India while enjoying an epic tale of adventure and love. Vayu Naidu's rendition is a masterful retelling that beautifully bridges the past and present, making the story of Rama and Sita relevant and inspiring for today's readers. The detailed descriptions of the forests, the divine encounters and the climactic battle against Ravana are both thrilling and thought-provoking. This book not only entertains but also imparts valuable lessons on leadership, morality and the importance of preserving the balance of nature. It reminds us of the timeless values of humility, respect for all life and the power of resilience'—Nikil Shyam Sunder, 2022 Emmy Award winner of *McEnroe vs McEnroe*

THE
LIVING LEGEND

RAMAYANA TALES FROM
FAR AND NEAR

VAYU NAIDU

EBURY
PRESS

An imprint of Penguin Random House

EBURY PRESS

Ebury Press is an imprint of the Penguin Random House group of companies
whose addresses can be found at global.penguinrandomhouse.com

Published by Penguin Random House India Pvt. Ltd
4th Floor, Capital Tower 1, MG Road,
Gurugram 122 002, Haryana, India

Penguin
Random House
India

First published in Ebury Press by Penguin Random House India 2024

Copyright © Vayu Naidu 2024

ISBN 9780143466031

Typeset in Adobe Caslon Pro by Manipal Technologies Limited, Manipal
Printed at Replika Press Pvt. Ltd, India

www.penguin.co.in

MIX
Paper | Supporting
responsible forestry
FSC™ C016779

For Gadadhar, the eternal storyteller

Contents

Kanda IV

Kanda V

Kanda VI

Kanda VII

Introduction

Easter Monday 2024

Dear reader,

As we know, there are many choices in *how* to read a book with multiple devices that are digital and tactile. We can recline, sit or stand, be stationary or listen or read while commuting. This is only possible with the gift of being able to read. In most media, we are given time options too. Between one to three minutes to pick the bites that can be read in the least amount of time to suit our shrinking attention span.

I think it's best you know the home truth about this one. This book is for young adults and older ones too. You can read this book in one 'shot'—as swift as an arrow making its mark. But the real adventure is how many questions you will start asking about how or what or why did the story take place the way it does. And that's the unmeasured time we will take to travel this living legend.

For me, these tales from the Ramayana appeared in the imagination like a cinema. When I first started listening to Storytellers and later started performing myself, I was 'reporting' from my inner eye with sound effects, dialogue, movement, gesture and the silence that followed. But something else was prodding me while I was absorbed by the telling of this vibrant story. The prod was beckoning me to figure out what was behind the cinematic experience. I enjoyed meeting the characters in the story and travelling with them across sandy, dry riverbeds and overflowing ones, blue hills, dense tropical forests, encountering the plant and animal realms, the ocean and shorelines, taking note of their adventures while experiencing what they learned from it. Their learning continues to have an impact on me, on you and those after us. How can that happen?

Originating in India, the Ramayana is compelling epic literature for its poetry attributed first to Valmiki (c. fourth century BCE) and all subsequent versions respond to new contexts across the geographical regions where storytellers travelled. The Ramayana was told and sung in regional dialects and languages by itinerant storytellers travelling across India. Festivals created infrastructures for pageants, at rituals in temples and in homes for celebrations, and the story was spread with interpolations. It also travelled across the seas with tradesmen and craftsmen to Southeast Asia. The Ramayana offers a complex matrix of statecraft, relationships between parents, siblings, men and women through its predominantly linear narrative. Significantly, more than in any other epic, the relationship between humans, animals and plants in the forest is very marked in my exploration of the Ramayana. Thus, it is the epic that travelled across land and sea, as metaphor and with migrants. In *The Living Legend*, every being is connected, sustaining the equilibrium of love as life between conflicting forces.

Humans are not the superior species. We see this with the counsel of Hanuman who is the erudite and wise vanara chief minister advising Rama in exile. Rakshasa-asura-demons are not homogeneously inclined towards heinous crimes as we see with the dedication of Vibhishana. The prosperity and sophistication of Ravana is mesmerizing. It is his uncontrollable desires that make him deviate from being an esteemed leader; his tragic flaw—greed.

The story is projected and viewed by our inner screen, of the life that they are living. Between the action and the plot, we are putting together what our identification with this story is: reconciliation of conflicting and painful opposites of love–hate, anger–peace and so on, in seeking a bridge to greater understanding about choice, responsibility and consequence; facing our demons and meeting our courage with humility and generosity from the constant factor—the constant that is the Truth against all odds from all perspectives.

You might ask, 'What is unique about the Ramayana' in this book?

No surprises. It is a story of the adventures of a young prince and how he is within a matrix of relationships with the love of his life, his wife Sita.. He fights for justice in a war, as we know through Puranic history is a compendium of oral tales functioning as chronicles. He takes it on as a fight for right against might.

In retelling this story, *The Living Legend* is drawn from resources within India and overseas from Southeast Asian cultures—Malaysia, Vietnam, Thailand, Cambodia, Myanmar, Sri Lanka—finding new meanings with craftsmen, sculptors, puppeteers, dancers and musicians. It has made us, tellers and writers, read and write, reaching different parts of the country and the world. The experiences of the characters are universal, even if drawn from local sources.

What are we celebrating in this festival of light? Diwali (or Deepavali) is now a global autumn festival. In the Indic imagination—folk or classical—lighting a lamp, or switching a string of lights on, is symbolic of an action or enactment of lighting that becomes a ritual. The action signifies layers of meaning and I'm listing them:

- seeing the light through the dark tunnel of fear and misery in troubling times;
- removing ignorance through knowledge;
- clearing a misunderstanding;
- being illumined.

This book shows us how truth can dispel the darkness of ignorance. It shows how one's word is to be honoured through action for harmony and balance.

In the story, Rama at sixteen is sought by Viswamithra, a great sage who has noted that in the Dandaka forest plant and animal life was contaminated by the rakshasas. Dandakaranya, or the Dandaka forest, is in the present-day map of India in the states of Chhattisgarh, Odisha, Telangana and Andhra Pradesh. It has dimensions of about 200 miles (320 km) from north to south and about 300 miles (480 km) from east to west.*

Vishwamitra travels by foot, with single-minded purpose to Ayodhya. King Dasaratha opens out every dimension of his wealth, treasure, status, dignity and propriety to welcome the solitary sage. King Dasaratha, waiting with anticipation, welcomes him with 'whatever your wish, that is my command'.

Walking into his kingdom, Viswamithra's response is: 'I want your son Rama to come with me into the forest where Tataka and other rakshasas are creating havoc. And if this is not contained at this stage, it could spread throughout the world.'

The word of honour is a very important decree and bond during the classical age of statecraft and in personal relationships. In fact, stories within Ramayana pivot on how to keep the *honour* of a word given, and how it sustains relationships and society. You will see how this happens throughout the story. What are the consequences when a word is withdrawn? It amounts to betrayal as we

---

* Stanley A. Wolpert, Muzaffar Alam, Joseph E. Schwartzberg, Sanat Pai Raikar, Romila Thapar, R. Champakalakshmi, T.G. Percival Spear, Sanjay Subrahmanyam, K.R. Dikshit, Frank Raymond Allchin, Philip B. Calkins and A.L. Srivastava, 'India'. *Encyclopedia Britannica*, 27 March 2024, https://www.britannica.com/place/India. Accessed 1 April 2024.

see how Queen Kaikeyi and King Dasaratha react to a 'forgotten' promise. It creates toxicity, having repercussions on all society; the world order becomes corrosive, and we see Vibhishana, despite being Ravana's brother, advising against the king's, his brother's, wishes in Lanka.

Viswamithra reads the expression on Dasaratha's face. Rama was a long-awaited son, the eldest and most favoured, and primed to lead the dynasty. For Dasaratha, it is the future of the kingdom, the world, through his son.

For Viswamithra, Rama contains extraordinary power which is untainted by ambition. Rama may not know this. He is a teenager. For Dasaratha, Rama is *his* sixteen-year-old son, who was born following a great yagna, ritual sacrifice, propitiated by yoga and Rishi Rishyasringa.

Sage Vashistha, at a later stage, comes into one of the parallel stories (not in this book) of the Ramayana, when Rama, as a teenager, wishes to renounce the kingdom and seek the absolute truth as pure consciousness known as Brahman. It is all-pervasive, existing in the moment as we are: Brahman. In my words, I feel this consciousness is above, below, around, beyond and through, and near and here and is present, constantly. There is a scriptural text with commentary that fills one with wonder. It is translated as *Nectar of Supreme Knowledge: Yoga Vashistha Sarah*. It is an original Bengali translation (1968) by Swami Dhiresananda, of the Ramakrishna and Vivekananda Order of monks. A translation (2023) by Swami Sarvadevananda was brought to my attention by Swami Sarvapriyananda, resident minister and spiritual leader of the Vedanta Society of New York, in his lectures. By drawing attention to the evidence in the text, Vashishta, a wise sage is guiding a young Rama about pure consciousness. Rama, comprehending this higher truth, is disenchanted by the material world around him and wants to seek this pure consciousness in secluded landscapes. Vashishta, having given Rama a taste of that higher truth, has to also persuade Rama to understand that consciousness is immanent. The sage has no material possessions, his student is an heir apparent to a kingdom. The text and its nectar of knowledge combine in the genius of a true teacher. Swami Sarvapriyananda, in his exposition, bridges the original context of an epic age with relevance to the contemporary listener's daily reality in the twenty-first century.

An inspirational dialogue, repartee even, it is a discourse on how Sage Vashishta asks the teenage Rama: 'Where will you go to seek the Truth? It is all here. It is this, it is here, it is now and it is That. And you are 'That' (paraphrase mine). Where can we go to seek this horizon? It is the question we too ask ourselves.

Vashistha is balancing the tidal empathy factor that is suffused by Brahman, pure consciousness. Rakshasas could be unempathetic. Rama is empathetic, but the balance of knowing when to act and for what purpose and making the right choice are the crux of the discourse; the premise of being empowered when you feel powerless and how to practise it.

It forms the mahakavya '*Tat tvam asi*, or *aham Brahmasmi*'. 'I' is not the little individual 'I' limited to body and mind. But pure spirit that resides in the body—'I am that, pure consciousness full of light'. That was something Viswamithra could see radiating in Rama—the light of pure consciousness.

What is consciousness, which in the Yoga Vasistha Sarah, as explicated to us, is an analogy. A vast, still, calm lake. In that, everything is reflected. People walking past and chattering. The birds swoop and the fish radiate rings and bubbles of oxygen in the water as they leap to catch the hovering insects caught by the light of the sun. The mirror-like lake reveals a storm through the trees, and even the trembling leaves are reflected. It is an idea where the analogy enables all the senses and rasa (essence or emotive intelligence) of wonder, love, disgust, heroism, pathos, laughter, anger, fear and peace in the characters, played out through the stories. But the observer (or the witness or the listener) is urged to see that all the images on the lake, like the stories we listen to from the Ramayana, catching their excitement and anticipation, the lake (or the canvas or the screen) holding all this, is eternal and constant. It enables us to witness. The reader (or the listener) is a witness learning from the actions of the characters played out, understanding the significance of action and consequence in the moment of heightened crisis.

I have enjoyed bringing to the fore the emphasis on the environment, not as a trend but as a unique dimension in the Ramayana, establishing a relationship with nature. Too often, we have been caught by the internal drama of the characters, but the living and legendary quality of the stories here is their ability to explain the dependence and interrelations between animal forces and plant forces. The forces that come together to accomplish the release of Sita from captivity, the herb Sanjivini, the armies of monkeys, bears, turtles, even squirrels, building the bridge across the ocean from coast to coast.

The rishis were advisers to kings, and some were kings who gave up their kingdom to become rishis. The stories bring together their observations of the ecosystem and eyewitness accounts of changes in the bend of the river, migratory patterns of birds, spawning sanctuaries within the forest, and the emergence of elements creating imbalances in clouds and rain. Today, we understand it as data and analysis and brand it as climate change. It was everyone's responsibility to treat the environment with respect, a code of behaviour that made a kingdom prosperous by its harvests, ensuring the elements were worshipped, fulfilling the rituals with fire and culminating in feeding the ancestors, community and progeny—past, present and future. The fire sacrifices (or performing *yagnas*) were worshipful due to the interconnectedness of the elements, earth, sentient beings, communities, and the individual as a heterogenous yet cumulative part of the Self.

The pivot and advent to the making of Rama is the invitation to Dandaka forest; a metaphoric space we enter with him, where his quest is pure. He faces his fear and with his beating heart seeks the light that reveals the truth of the oneness of multiple voices.

At the centre is a beating heart of connectivity, the heartbeat of all living beings. The connectivity has a biological manifestation. All living beings have cells, each cell has mitochondria that is the energy source for the development of the body—plants, animals and humans.* Even as we all share this, we are mutating to evolve. It is in this sense of connectedness in all living beings that we understand that our diversities in all forms unite and are experienced as an amalgam of one. This includes backstories, past lives and the different worlds of gods, demons, humans and animals. The focus is on the interconnectedness of the non-linear entities, in circles, spirals and all trajectories possible, converging at one point. That is how this is a living epic celebrated during Deepavali, releasing people who listen from fear, anxiety, pride, jealousy and negative energies, while endorsing positive energies of courage, humility, hard work and generosity, which makes it a living legend (or immortal).

I've endeavoured to express some thoughts about what inspired me to write this book for young adults and old ones too, and about how it provided a lens through which so much became clearer in seeing the 'light' that reaches all parts of the globe. This epic draws the mind and unfolds the meaning of connectedness with life in its diversity. As Vashishtha instructed Rama in the light of consciousness, the story is what we experience in our daily responsibility to life and all that is around us in times of love and war. I close with what I think is best expressed

---

* https://www.mrc-mbu.cam.ac.ukhttp://www.mrc-mbu.cam.ac.uk/

in a Sangam Tamil poem on love and war, translated by
A.K. Ramanujan:

Earth's bounty
Bless you, earth,
field,
forest,
valley,
or hill,
you are only as good
as the good young men
in each place.*

---

* *The Four Hundred Songs of War and Wisdom: An Anthology of Poems from
Classical Tamil, the Purananuru*
George L. (tr.) Hart and Hank Heifetz (tr.)
Hart, George L. (tr.); Hank Heifetz (tr.);*The Four Hundred Songs of War
and Wisdom: An Anthology of Poems from Classical Tamil, the Purananuru*,
(Columbia University Press, p. 159).

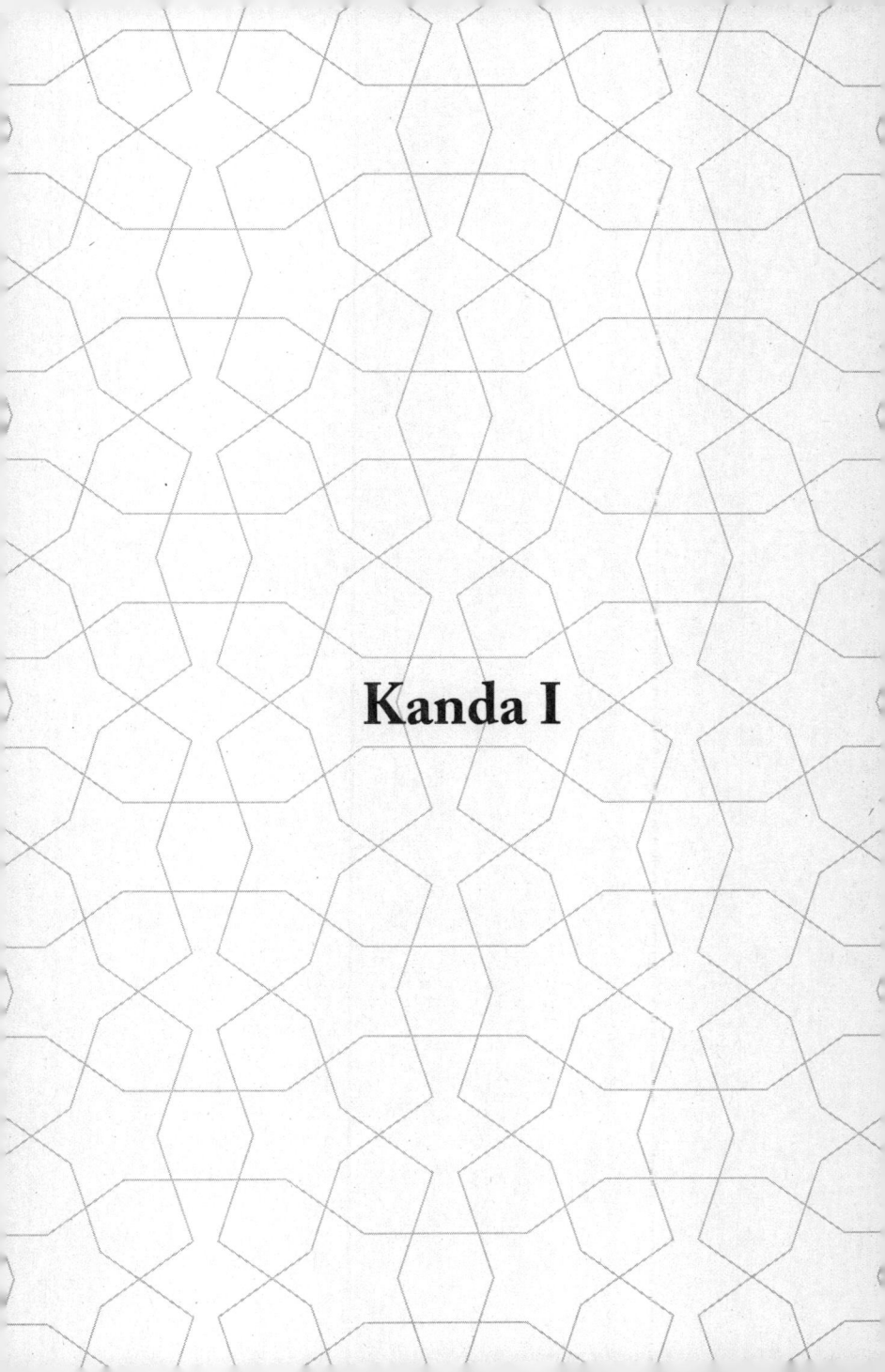

Kanda I

1

A Story in Search of an Author

400 BCE, Kosala by the Sarayu

Midnight. A short shower of rain. The warm air filled with the rising smell of the moist, red earth. In the distance, the sound of hoof beats. It was moving closer. Suddenly, a sliver of the scythe-shaped moon peeped through the smothering clouds. In the flickering moonlight, a shining dot could be seen gliding down the forest pathway.

If you blinked, the dot would enlarge. It was luminous in the watery moonlight. As it drew closer, you could recognize it was a white horse. Soon, its hooves were thundering on the path by the bank of the River Sarayu. You dared not stand in its path. There was every chance of you being flattened! But more importantly, you had to let the horse gallop on, without stopping.

Why? Well, if you have lived in that time, you would have known that this was the Aswamedha. It was a ritual/ceremony conducted by a King, often on the advice of his sages and ministers, to assert his sovereignty over his lands and kingdoms, allies or vassal states. If the King had acquired prosperity and security for his subjects, he was encouraged to offer protection to the neighbouring kingdoms by asserting that he was the 'King of Kings'. In the ritual, a white horse from the royal stables would be set free to gallop across other kingdoms to assert the originator king's power to gain territory. If the horse was captured in any kingdom, then it meant the king's authority was challenged. The horse had been sent out from the kingdom of Kosala by King Dasaratha of the Ikshvaku clan. This clan of warriors were the descendants of the solar race, and the ancient lawgiver Manu. Dasaratha, 'the one who steers ten chariots together', was a great warrior as well as an astute politician. He had been advised by the sages and ministers and some diplomatic envoys of the neighbouring kingdoms to declare himself the 'King of Kings'. He was known to be the 'Grand Protector' of his people, as well as of the smaller kingdoms around Kosala.

Dasaratha was a renowned conqueror, one who followed the laws of dharma, and his kingdom was as prosperous as it was hospitable. He could do no wrong in his peoples' eyes; he believed that the protection of the forests, where sages and wild animals lived, was far more important than having an army. This idea was exceedingly popular among his subjects. The sages living in the forests practised deep meditation and so they developed an extrasensory perception. They observed nature and took note of changing patterns in the environment. They understood subtle changes in the air and could detect shape-shifting rakshasas who wanted to terrorize nature. The king and his people believed that protecting the sages and the forests, where they lived, led to bountiful harvests, and an increase in trade and wealth in the treasury. It was a simple and successful formula: health, employment and refinement through philosophy and the arts equalled a wealthy kingdom.

The capital city of Kosala was Ayodhya, meaning 'that which cannot be subdued by war'. The rivers Gomati, Tamasa and Sarayu braided their way around the kingdom and were worshipped as goddesses because they were the source of life for plants, animals and humans. The rivers also acted as a protective embankment against potential invaders. It's not as though there was no poverty, but even poor people in Kosala felt they belonged to an order where they were looked after. In fact, if you were to elect a king, Dasaratha would win every time. Every evening, in a gathering of households, lamps were lit and incense burned, and a storyteller would tell stories of courage, of armies led by Dasaratha, how he had won the hearts of his queens—there were three of them—how he loved them and how they loved him in return, and of his patronage of the arts. Every heart in the kingdom longed to listen to these ever-expanding stories that grew like branches of trees.

When he had sent the Aswamedha out, it meant that all the kings, through whose lands the horse had galloped, willingly consented to Dasaratha being crowned the King of Kings. If the horse was captured, or stolen, then Dasaratha would have to go to that kingdom with his armies to avenge the crime. If the horse was not returned following a peaceful discussion, or indeed a confrontation, then Dasaratha would have to prove his might. That meant war. But we don't have to go that far, yet! This is the story of the future, and for the present, peace holds the river of human emotions safely within its banks.

Let's go back in time. Many years before this happened, in a part of this forest where the Aswamedha was to gallop, there lived a monstrous criminal. His name was Ratnakar. He made a living by capturing travellers, robbing them of all their belongings, and quite often killing them so that no one could report him. What was worse, he was not insane. He just decided to be 'king of the jungle'. He even had a family. He supported his father and mother in addition to his wife and many, many children. The funny thing was that they never really knew what he did to keep them fed and clothed. He never told them where he went out to work, or how long he would be gone or what kind of job he did, and they never asked him about it. Life seemed just fine when they avoided those awkward questions.

One afternoon, even though the sun was high and hot in the subcontinent, this part of the forest was dark and deep. There were amlaka shrubs with many branches splayed out like a tiger's paws growing close between trees. Amlaka's bark could be used to make a dye, and the shrub had poisonous fruits that spat dark stains on the forest floor. There were mango trees, and the nimba, whose leaves were chewed at funerals. Entwining these were the patala, evergreen, climbing, weaving between trees and shrubs, creating dungeons of darkness in the forest. It acted as a fortress for Ratnakar. He could spy on who or what was coming that way, while he could remain hidden. There was a forked path that formed the crossroads where unseasoned travellers would stop before proceeding north or south. This forked path was the trap and those travellers were Ratnakar's victims.

That afternoon, Sage Narada was walking through the forest. He was well known for his storytelling. He had often dined with the gods in a parallel world called Devaloka. He knew their local gossip—who was the celebrity of the month, whose palace was more stylish, who was the architect and interior designer, what were the new musical ragas and talas, who were the award-winning composers and dancers, most sought-after goddesses and celestial courtesans, who were the new mortals* allowed to entertain at the weddings. As marriages are made in heaven, the gods constantly had wedding parties. Narada was always invited because he was a journalist of mythology and knew his way into the many universes, or should I say of deva, bharatha and bhuta— gods–humans–animals–plants–elements and demons.

---

* Mortal/s is used when referring to humans who enter metaphorical landscapes such as heaven/Devaloka, or paradise, in relation to mythical beings such as gods/devas, etc. The term human/s is used as a physiological condition, and as potential prey in relation to wild animals or demons, or indeed other humans with demonic traits. These terms are used with a sense of irony about the categorization of qualities and the codification of class.

Beyond Devaloka, Narada also had meetings with the Greats—Brahma the creator, who was in the ether and could see north, south, east and west all at once; Vishnu, the life-sustaining spirit of the universe, who sat on a serpent with a hundred benign heads at the centre of the ocean; and Shiva, the dark-destroyer of stupidity, who was occasionally sighted at the Himalayas. Of these, Vishnu was a particularly special friend of Narada's. From gazing and wondering at the Greats, as we would the stars and constellations, Narada was in tune with the pulse of life. He spoke in a gentle timbre with music in his words. When he smiled, he lit the space around him, and when he walked, there was a gentle perfume of morning *mallika* jasmine around him.

He was chanting the one thousand and one names of Vishnu, the qualities of life, as he walked through this forest. The air was so thick you could cut it with a knife. Something rustled behind him. Before he could turn, someone leapt out of the bushes screaming, 'Come aaaaaaaaawwwwwwwnn! Give me all you've got or die!'

With these violent words, the face that spat them out was angry with eyes like red hot coals, hair and fingernails like tusks. The tip of his spear, aimed at Narada's head, quivered like a tongue dipped in blood. It was Ratnakar.

Everything about him spelt hatred and the will only to kill. What a state to be in!

Narada must have blinked, but he continued to smile his golden smile and said, 'Ah! Ratnakar, the famous King of the Jungle! What a rare privilege to catch sight of you!'

Ratnakar only let out a low growl: 'Aeee! Enuff of yer *buk-buk*! You will look and taste like a trapped chicken once I've wrung your neck. Out with it! All the things you've got!'

'Look my friend, as you can see, I have a bare torso and feet. I have nothing for you to loot and plunder like all the other travellers who have been passing through this forest,' said Narada calmly.

But Ratnakar was unconvinced. His eyes squirmed suspiciously as he said, 'Eeeeeeenough of that . . . I can sssee by your face, you have treasure as large as the worrrld.' A terrifying pause followed as he edged closer and whispered mercilessly, 'Hhhhhhaven't you?'

Another pause while Ratnakar took a breath from hissing.

Narada waited, almost as if to clear the air of the waves of violent sound before he answered in a sweet tone that rang like the chime of a prayer bell: 'You are a real soul searcher Ratnakar! Not many would have realized that a man like me, without any possessions, does have a treasure.' The lilt of his words, the way his eyes looked straight at Ratnakar, was as if ripples of calm were cleansing that forest, infested with years of dark human deeds. 'Yes, I might have the treasure of the world,' Narada said candidly, 'and you can have it too. But I will make a bargain with you. Why don't you go and ask your family this question: "Would you die in my stead and take with you *my* sins upon your head?" Look, you have sacrificed so much for your family, to give them all the wealth and prosperity that they want, without a thought for yourself. Come back with an answer and let us take it from there.'

Ratnakar laughed. 'What cheek!' he thought. But he couldn't help noting how Narada was completely calm and composed. Ratnakar decided this man was a match for him, not a victim. It would be fantastic to play his game and teach this well-educated poet whom life and people had treated well a real lesson. What else was there to do that afternoon? This little game would pass the time and then, in any case, he would get the treasure of the world from this man. Ratnakar was also sure that his family would die for him because he had given them so much.

So he tied Narada to one of the aerial roots of a banyan tree, making sure that the ropes cut tight into his ankles and wrists so that even if he tried to wriggle free, it would hurt so much that he would scream and Ratnakar could return to finish him off. Ratnakar went with a superior air, and a strut in his step to prove Narada wrong.

He knew his way well in those dungeons of foliage. He came to the clearing where he had built his tree houses. Narada's question was playing like a nursery rhyme in his head. It had a jingle to it. The first one of his family he found was his father lying in the hammock and having a leisurely afternoon smoke.

He said, 'Father, would you die in my stead and take with you, my sins, upon your head?' His father almost catapulted out of the hammock and said, 'Whattt! How strange you are! Don't you know it is a privilege for you to look after me, after all those years I cared for you?

Remember, if it wasn't for me, you wouldn't even have been born!'

'Oh,' thought Ratnakar, 'that is the way fathers talk,' and went to look for his beloved mother.

She had just finished her afternoon meal and opened the box that Ratnakar had gifted to her just the day before after stealing it and killing a bridal procession. She had gasped with delight at all the diamonds and gold that were in it. 'My loving son, *kanna*! You are my favourite! None of the other children have shown me such love the way you have. Diamonds are truly a woman's best friend!' Now, when he came to her, she placed her hands on him as he lowered his head to be blessed and kissed by her. Ratnakar thought, 'What a world of difference between fathers and mothers!' So, with a beaming smile, showing all his betel nut and tobacco-stained teeth, he asked, 'Mother, you have always loved me. Would you die in my stead and take with you all *my* sins upon your head?'

Her hands placed lovingly on his head now turned into fists to pummel him. She began screaming, 'Aiyiyooooooo! My son wants me to die before him! What did I give birth to? Are you a human or has some hideous spirit come to haunt me? Aiyiyooooooo!' and continued wailing.

'Bad timing to ask her a question like that just after her birthday,' thought Ratnakar as he fled from her in search of his wife.

He loved his wife passionately and she loved him too. And she had given him many, many children. She was inside the house, sweeping the floor after the sumptuous

lunch of fried goat's brain, wild boar trotter curry, peacock
pilau and milky sweets stolen from the wedding party
that he had the day before. He went to her and raised her
from the floor by her shoulders. Her eyes were shyly cast
downward, while a smile curled upwards on her young
and shining face. She always smelt so sweet and loved her
husband's caresses. He held her within a breath's space and
whispered, 'Ah! I love you so much. You are everything
that is dearest to me. Tell me, will you die in my stead and
take *my* sins upon your head?' Suddenly her eyes flashed
lightning and pummelling him with her fists, she stormed
at him, 'How dare you! Since when have you started this
kind of talk? Do you want me to die and our children to
be eaten by wild animals while you are hunting for food?
Cheee! What nonsense! Why should I care what sins you
have on your head? I don't care what you do for a living as
long as we get the money to feed and clothe our children!'

Even if you were there, you wouldn't have heard it. But a
tiny volcano exploded in Ratnakar's heart and another inside
his head. Ratnakar was a broken man. He was so sure that
his entire family would die for him but, as it turned out,
they neither loved him, nor cared for him. He discovered
they only cared for themselves and that he was, in fact, their
slave. Somehow he gathered himself, held his head high and
walked back like the living dead to where Narada was tied.

Narada tenderly said, 'I know from your face what the
answer is. You have abandoned your family because they
do not want to make the sacrifice you have made for them.
Now I must keep my part of the bargain.'

Ratnakar untied him. Narada gently rubbed his wrists to renew his blood circulation. He picked up a fallen leaf, and with his right thumbnail he wrote a word. He folded it neatly as we would a precious letter. He touched Ratnakar on the shoulder and said, 'Don't despair Ratnakar; even if everything in the world has deserted you, there is a presence within you that will never leave you. It is a constant source of light. When the right time comes, you will open the leaf. Read that word with care. Remember to repeat it with concentration. Now, if you will let me, I must go.' And with that, Narada once again started recounting the thousand and one names of Vishnu, the life-giver, the lotus lidded, the love of life.

As Narada moved into the dark tunnel of amlaka trees in the forest, Ratnakar saw a gentle halo around the man and for just a moment, his smile had left an island of peace in Ratnakar's heart.

When Narada had completely disappeared from sight, Ratnakar returned to himself, and discovered he was furious. He had abandoned his family because they could not give him the love he wanted and now, he was stuck in this forest. Besides, he was hungry. Not a single traveller had passed his way to loot and plunder and worse still, not even a wild animal was around that he could barbeque and eat. The hunger was growling in his stomach and as it grew louder, so did his anger and frustration. Many hours passed and when he was feeling a little faint, he noticed the leaf. 'When the time is ripe . . .' Narada's voice rippled across his memory. So, he picked up the leaf as if it was a dangerous weapon that would explode if handled badly. He opened it. The simple word hit him hard. 'MA-RA'.

'Aiyooooooooooooooo!' Ratnakar bayed like a wounded animal. The sound echoed through the forest. For, he knew the word MARA meant 'the world', meaning society, civilization and everything associated with it.

'Mara! Mara! What good has the world done for me? Look at the world . . . I am imprisoned in this forest; I have been cut off from all civilization . . . I do not even have the dignity of a wild beast to roam free. And that man has cheated me . . . he has given me just this word.' Ratnakar raged against himself, he cursed and spat. His language was foul. But every time he paused to take a breath, the soothing voice of Narada echoed in his head. Narada had told him to repeat the word MARA with concentration. Ratnakar tried . . . Mara, Mara, Mara . . . He sounded like a crow. It sounded coarse. But he sat down cross-legged, and this time, closing his eyes, and concentrating on that word Mara, he repeated it in one breath: MaramaRamaramaramaRamaRama RamaRamaRamaRamaRamaRama . . .

He realized that from one word, another was emerging, like a tiny shoot from a seed. He concentrated even harder and the waves of sound from the new word 'Rama' illumined his imagination. Now, Ratnakar could see into the future. It was not some dark unknown void. He could see with his inner sight, as clearly as in sunlight, a youth named Rama.

Rama was yet to be born, but Ratnakar could see that his life was to be so inspiring, because in spite of all the struggles he was to face, there would always be something

so tender in his presence that it shone on his face, radiant
like the cool blue halo of the full moon. His very name
had changed the course of Ratnakar's life. A murderer
was now able to experience the gift of life. Could just a
word hold so much power? Could it be so uplifting that
it could help one rise from the deepest, darkest despair? Is
that what Narada could see in a monstrous criminal like
Ratnakar? The gift of light in the human spirit? Stars burn
so bright even though they are millions of miles away. So
even the goodness in a human being can radiate across
time and space. Surely, it wasn't that incredible! So many
questions were flying through Ratnakar's mind. Something
told him to concentrate on the light he could see within
himself and he held on to that instruction or perhaps it
was intuition, in the dark forest. Night came, and when
day broke, it was still dark in that forest, but Ratnakar
was so rapt in concentration, he did not move. Hours fled
into days, nights and weeks, the weeks became months,
and years passed. People walked peacefully through the
forest now because no attack had been reported for many
years. Everyone was relieved that maybe Ratnakar had
died. Nobody bothered to look out for him. And nobody
noticed that at the old crossroads, there was a huge anthill.
Ratnakar had sat motionless, concentrating on Rama, and
over the years, ants had built a hill over him.

Many, many years later, as some hermits were passing
by, and clearing away some of the poisonous plants to let
daylight into the forest, they saw human hair at the top
of the anthill. On opening a small part of it, so as not

to disturb the ants, they discovered a man, alive, but so deep in concentration that he was not disturbed by them. So they named him 'VALMIKI', one who has so much concentration, that he has given up consciousness of time, and an anthill could grow upon his head.

After many more years, Ratnakar opened his eyes. And it was true, he could see into the future. He could see into the life of a youth called Rama, how in an age of darkness, he brought a tiny spark of light. But however much Valmiki wanted to express the story, he felt he was so infected by his life as Ratnakar, that to tell Rama's story would be to soil that name. In his shame, Valmiki decided to take an oath of silence. Not a sound slipped from his lips for years.

Many years later, as he was walking through the forest, he saw the bright yellow crests of two Krauncha* herons mating. The poet in him experienced joy from their abandon and pleasure. It exhilarated him so much that he continued to marvel at the sight. Suddenly, something whistled past him. It was a hunter's swift arrow. It struck the male bird's breast and stained his yellow feathers with its ruby-red blood. The female Krauncha hovered around, screeching at the tragic loss of a male companion. Possibly more than that, she lamented the loss of pleasure.

Valmiki also screamed out as if the pain was his own. He cursed the hunter and his livelihood, 'You have snatched the very joy of life in the moment of its making;

---

* Hari Prasad Shastri, trans., *The Ramayana of Valmiki* (London: Shanti Sadan, 1952), p.10.

Hear this! You will never know it and never return to the forest!' Valmiki was surprised at his outburst. He, who had taken an oath to never speak, feeling the living bird's loss at the tragic death of its love and lover, broke his silence. Valmiki's grief spilled out as a sound. He had uttered a verse, each of equal syllables, which could be sung to the veena. He realized life holds out two hands offering us growth. Separation and loss are a part of human life, edged with happiness and laced with sadness. Happiness makes us move forward, sadness offers us the time for reflection. He realized too that every joy is followed by sorrow and life only remains constant by continuously changing.

Valmiki washed himself in the river. That night, as he sat by a pool of water, the moon was reflected in it, and it was as radiant as the face of Rama. He began to compose the first of the 24,000 slokas that are the 48,000 lines of what lives on today as Valmiki's Ramayana.

Many sages and storytellers continue to tell this story, embellishing it with the tributes and torment of their times, but never forgetting that the struggle to triumph over the force of darkness with the force of light is an eternal fight. And so . . . on with the story written in this time.

2

The Bridge between Longing and Fulfilment

Valmiki heard the verse drumming in his head. He could see clearly into the future to that hazy-moon night. The Aswamedha horse's hooves were pounding towards the gates of Kosala. The cheers from the crowds were rising in waves of chants as it galloped closer to the finishing point. It meant that no other king had challenged the might of Dasaratha. Valmiki could hear the cheering of the sages, ministers, generals, merchants, agriculturalists and labourers; the loyal subjects proclaiming: 'DASA-RA -THA! KING OF KINGS!'

The horse was reined in at a large enclosure at the banks of the River Sarayu. The sacrificial altar for the horse was built in the shape of an eagle. The most celebrated sage of the time, Rishyasringa, was invited from the land of Anga

to conduct the ceremony. While Dasaratha felt humbled
by the honour given to him by his people, he was also
anxious that all the rituals for the ceremonial sacrifice of the
horse went according to scripture. The horse was a symbol
of the King's power by the consent of the neighbouring
kingdoms. Now that it had run the earth, it was being
prepared for a yagna, a sacrifice, as a gift to the elements
who were worshipped as gods for prosperity.

Dasaratha had a special request, in fact, an appeal, to
make to the elements and the guardian spirits or gods who
ruled over them. He wanted an heir to his kingdom. He
had three wives whom he loved dearly and each of them
loved him in her unique way, befitting her nature. But none
of them could give him a child. He had everything in this
world except the one thing he and his wives wanted so
much—children.

So Dasaratha decided to organize a prayer ritual to ask
for children, following the horse's sacrifice. He was anxious
that everything and everyone connected with the sacred
rituals was perfect. There were so many eminent sages who
lived in the forests around his kingdom, so, why had he
invited Rishyasringa from Anga to be the master of rituals?
What was so special about him?

Rishyasringa, like Narada, the sage of Valmiki's youth,
had the ability to live in parallel worlds. While Narada
composed songs of love and faith, that we know as bhakti,
he talked, walked and ate with the gods most of the time.
Rishyasringa, however, lived in the world of men and
women almost all of the time. He had the gift of looking

into people's past lives. It was a kind of X-ray vision; he could see beyond the mere bones of a human, and into the very marrow of human nature; what made someone easy to be with, others miserable company, and in some, the strong desire to harm others. This let Rishyasringa see clearly why people were in the situation they were, in their present life. He knew the part Dasaratha was to play in the great game of creation. This was serious stuff and would change the destiny of the world.

Rishyasringa could see the flames from the altar rising like a winged messenger from the belly of the earth to the sky. At the auspicious hour of the ritual, it was still dark. It had to be, because the time that the gods watch over the world is four o'clock in the morning. It is also the hour of our deepest rest, when our imagination and gods are at play. The sage could see the flames rise, like a chord of hope rising from human chants to the gods in the heavens.

At that very moment, the *deva*s, or the 'shining ones', were having a conference and were gathered outside Brahma's assembly hall. Devaloka is made up of gods or shining ones, and then the top or Maha Gods, whom I call the Greats—Brahma, Vishnu and Shiva. At the time of the Aswamedha, while Rishyasringa was watching the flames from the altar on earth reaching for the heavens, or Vaikunta, Vishnu was in a high-security, top-secret discussion with Brahma. A new situation had arisen that was to spell the fate of the world.

After the Big Bang and the creation of the universe, there was a time of famine and drought, brought on by neglect. Some of the gods turned into ferocious and ever-hungry creatures that became the ogres, monsters and demons known as *asuras*. In time, Ravana, the descendent of an ogre, conquered all the other asuras. He then prayed fervently to Shiva for a boon, which is really a very special wish. It was not a simple prayer said while bending on a knee with folded hands. To make a special wish, Ravana had to do something spectacular. Only he could; he was strong, skilful and brave and also deeply misunderstood, which made him very lonely. He wanted to be noticed. So, he hung upside down from a tree over a fire and thought of nothing and no one else except Shiva for forty years. He wasn't noticed. So he decided to climb down. From below, he saw that the gods were a little worried about crossing the bridge between Devaloka and the human world, as a serpent was threatening them from crossing. The gods didn't want to get their hands, silks, crowns and jewels dirty, so Ravana decided to help them and killed the serpent. Finally, he had a vision of Shiva. Shiva, the Great, was delighted by his penance and asked him what he wished. Ravana replied, 'I wish for immortality. You know what I mean. Life, forever and ever!'

Shiva simply said: 'Sorry, most-competent-of-all-asuras, but you can't have it. It's reserved. Your labours to achieve my attention have been seriously impressive. But so sorry. Some are immortal. Unfortunately, you aren't.'

Ravana would not accept disappointment. He huffed and he puffed, big smoky coils of his fury were flying out from him like clouds of stinging mosquitoes. Then, he asked the Great Shiva if he could be made invincible against the gods so that none could injure or kill him. It seemed a fair deal. Shiva, always known for his generosity, was pleased with what seemed Ravana's compromise and the wish was granted.

Ravana was given the beautiful island of Lanka to rule. He ruled well, became terrifyingly powerful and was a law unto himself. His art of magic and cloning of the existing worlds began to trouble the gods. And thanks to Shiva, no one, not even Indra, the chieftain of the devas and godfather of the heavens, could find a strategy that would keep Ravana under check. The fate of the heavens was at stake because Ravana was beginning to invade peoples' minds with dreams, of power in pursuit of personal gain, even if it harmed others. This brought in its wake, greed, conquest and discontent, and a disregard for humanity. It was the reversal of aspiration, achievement and fulfilment; a profound ideal that was the essence of being human. This was why the devas had gathered outside Brahma's Assembly Hall. They wanted to know the antidote to Shiva's boon of near immortality that had been granted to Ravana.

Down on earth, Rishyasringa was placing sacred barks and twigs dipped in pure ghee, as oblation on the ritual fire, while in Devaloka, Brahma waited breathlessly for Vishnu's decision.

Vishnu had a charming smile as he said, 'You mean . . . Ravana is causing all this . . . by himself?'

Brahma was embarrassed. He coughed slightly. On earth, it caused rolling thunder in the sky. He knew what Vishnu was suggesting. What were the devas doing, indulging in all the luxury of heaven, and their immortality, neglecting people, while one asura had such amazing power to destroy the universe? Brahma admitted, to himself, that it was time he made cuts on some executive privileges of the devas. 'Well . . . er, hmmm . . .' was all he could say.

Shiva had just entered the Great Assembly Hall. He was frowning. Nandi, his wise old bull, who accompanied him everywhere, was fidgety and whisked his tail. It got entangled in Shiva's cascading locks of hair. 'How many times do I have to tell you not to do that?' Shiva said to Nandi. 'Well, I think it's time you had a haircut, and I think it's time you took some responsibility for all this mess the whole world is in!' came Nandi's sharp reply.

'Order! Order!' said Brahma, 'the devas are waiting for us to do something about creation, Dasaratha is holding a yagna sacrifice calling on the gods to give . . .'

'Are you all blaming me?' asked Shiva genuinely perplexed. He looked at Nandi and said, 'I had nothing to do with it. Ravana worked very hard to contact me. Not only that, he showed such promise. He's bright, hands-on and doesn't leave the hard work for others. He has spectacular ideas, and he knows how to make them happen—'

'But surely,' Nandi cut in, 'you must screen *who* you grant boons to and have some thought about what *kind* of boons you grant!'

Vishnu was listening, and with his mischievous smile he said: 'I remember how Ravana taunted me in the last encounter.' 'Yes,' Shiva said eagerly, having found an ally, 'that's right, Vishnu, you tell them. When Ravana was in the form of Nandaka and got a little out of hand about the immortality business, I did try to burn him with my third eye. Didn't I? Just tell them!'

'Yes,' said Nandi a little cheekily, 'you're so generous about keeping your promises; you gave him a diamond finger so that he could kill anything and anyone just by pointing it.'

'He threatened everyone, even the gods!' said Brahma. 'Thank goodness Vishnu had the good sense to enchant him as a female dancer and . . .'

'Yes, that was super!' said Shiva, who is also the creator of dance, 'you got him to copy all your movements and then pointed your finger to your thigh and when he did the same . . . Ba-buh-bah-Booommm! He exploded!' They all laughed uproariously. On earth, thunder rolled, lightning hissed and the wind howled.

Meanwhile, Rishyasringa dipped the sacred Kusha grass in the sacred *loshta* vessel and raised it to the heavens in an urgent prayer for divine intervention. The sacred flames grew higher.

Brahma, Vishnu and Shiva could feel the amber glow of its warmth. The laughter subsided. Vishnu said, 'It is time. When I destroyed Ravana last time, he mocked me, saying I deceived him as a woman and it wasn't fair. Now I must fight him as a man.'

Nandi sighed.

'I will be born as Dasaratha's son,' said Vishnu decisively.

Brahma and Shiva embraced their friend and speaking as one, said, 'You will forget where you have come from. You will fight with the heart and mind of a man. Our energy is always there for us to discover. It will help you triumph. Never forget, every cell of creation, every atom of being, is light. Keep truth and love as your weapons against the dark forces of delusion in the world. That will make everything return to light, where everything belongs. Remember, you are not alone.'

Some of the brighter gods who had gathered outside were able to tune into the frequency of airwaves that Brahma and Shiva were speaking in. They led the chorus:

'Truth Will Triumph with Light; Down with Delusion and Darkness; Truth Will Triumph with Light!'

On earth, the wind stopped howling. Everyone looked up; the clouds were clearing, and a soft amethyst glow spread across the sky. There was a short spell of rain from the departing clouds and then the warm, moist air filled with a scattering of fragrant *kannakambaram*, mallika petals and tulasi leaves. 'Very auspicious signs, a good omen!' the crowds of Ayodhya murmured.

At the ruby and emerald studded, eagle-shaped altar, Dasaratha sat, with his three wives on each side of the square fire altar. Agni, the fire Deva, was creating a bridge of flames rising like a golden chord of human hope between earth and Devaloka. Humans prayed to the Greats for fulfilment.

Dasaratha had been listening to all the sacred chants with concentration. When he had to offer his personal prayers, he washed his hands with the *gulak* water, and folded his palms. With eyes closed, he prayed with intense longing, and love, for a son and heir.

More sacred herbs, roots and fragmented barks of trees were delicately spun into the sacrificial fire. The golden flames began to rise even higher, gently at first, and then leaping upwards. Suddenly amid the flames, a golden figure appeared. Through the veil of orange fire, it looked at first like a lion sitting on its haunches. The fur and flames were of the same burnished gold. It roared within the blazing fire. As the flame diminished, the lion seemed to descend from the sky like a chariot of the devas. Soon, the lion became a goddess. She was dressed in gold, with rubies and sapphires glistening all about her neck, wrists, ears, head and feet. She was awe-inspiring. She held a golden bowl with a carved lid.

Dasaratha was dazed and speechless. He stood with hands outstretched to salute the goddess; instead, he found he was holding the golden bowl. It was not a figment of his imagination! When he looked again, the goddess had vanished, only the golden flames were visible; dancing, kissing and crackling.

As he held the precious bowl, he looked at Rishyasringa. Dasaratha did not want to do anything that would interfere with or disrespect the ritual. He was visibly trembling with excitement when he was signalled to open it. It was *payasam*, the food of the gods. It tasted like the organic nectar of goodness! He gave a ladle of it to his first wife Queen Kausalya. She tasted it, 'Ummm . . .' and with great dignity, ate the payasam. He then gave another ladleful to Queen Sumitra, his second wife 'Umm . . . this is out of the world', she couldn't help thinking. She wanted more, but Dasaratha was offering a ladle of the payasam to Queen Kaikeyi, his luscious third wife. Dasaratha could not resist the look in Queen Sumitra's twinkling smile and decided to give her what was remaining in the vessel. A few more ceremonies were conducted till the sun emerged like a vermilion dot on the forehead of the sky. It left a mark in the memory of everyone in Kosala for generations to come. The bridge of longing had been crossed; the king and his queens had arrived on the banks of fulfilment.

The Greats were still having their top security meeting, which had resulted in Vishnu going down to earth. Just outside the Great Assembly Hall, the Greats' wives, Saraswati, Lakshmi and Parvati were also at the gathering of the gods. Brahma loved his Saraswati for her wide knowledge and her rhythmical and clear words to define things, beings and situations. Here she was, listening to the devas talk about their suffering as a result of Ravana's masquerades. She was placing their grievances into categories and labelling them with observations so that if a trial were to be held, there would be a record of evidence to the crimes. In another part of the gathering, some goddesses were insinuating in their tone and Parvati was defending her Shiva. She was holding on to Ganesha, her son, so that he wouldn't get lost in this crowd of adult devas. He was busy rubbing his trunk and his belly. The devas had to be careful how they spoke to Parvati. She had rather extreme means of sorting out nuisances. Without a doubt, she was loved by all as a benign mother of humanity. But, in a flash, she could turn into Kali, a ferocious mother, if there was a threat to creation. She was reputed for matching a vicious asura in terror and strength, and finally killing him.

Ganesha suddenly saw his favourite aunt, Goddess Lakshmi. He waddled speedily to her side as she was offering a tray of heavenly laddus latticed with cardamom, roasted cashew nuts, ghee and honey. Lakshmi had brought these back to share as Vishnu and she had just returned from a timeshare on the ocean-of-consciousness holiday. Ganesha took her blessings and began taking and eating laddus with the speed and skill of a juggling dancer, bringing merriment to the gathering. Lakshmi was comforting those who had lost their health or wealth at the hands of Ravana. She admired the humility and courage that some of these devas showed in wanting to go down to earth as humans, animals, mountains or herbs; in short, anything, to restore safety and happiness in the world once again. But everyone was waiting to hear the decision of the Greats.

Suddenly, there was a big 'Twaaannnnnggggh!' It sounded like a gigantic string from a musical instrument. Everyone whirled around. A woman, one of Lakshmi's maid-of-honour came running in, wailing and spluttering, 'How could he! Oh! Whose face did I see this morning that such bad tidings should be heard! Please, all you devas and devis forgive me! I was only doing my duty to my Goddess Lakshmi, keeping trespassers out. And now, this . . . the curse . . . what will we ever do!' and on and on she wailed.* Everyone whirled around again to see Lakshmi's reaction. But she wasn't there! She had vanished.

In Kosala, people talked for months on end of the Aswamedha and the fire sacrifice to the devas. At the end of nine months, there was a grand celebration. Dasaratha's three wives gave birth to four sons. Kausalya gave birth to Rama, Sumitra who had twins (as she ate two portions of the payasam), gave birth to Lakshmana and Shatrughana, and Kaikeyi gave birth to Bharatha.

As these four young boys were growing up, their father proved to be not only a brave king, but a really good parent. He knew that the boys would be fussed over by their many mothers and the people of Ayodhya. He believed in giving them some ground rules, about education as knowledge, self-refinement, and statecraft as welfare of the people and state. Dasaratha decided that all his sons would not only be literary, but also be supple of body and skilled in martial arts. He engaged master musicians to teach them singing and composition, which would aid in thinking clearly and

---

* Narada curses Lakshmi to be born on earth as the daughter of an asura and to finally be the death of her father, because one of her attendants insults him. Source: Adbhuta Ramayana – Sanskrit as cited in Garrett's *Ramayana in the Arts of Asia*.

delivering their edicts with conviction when speaking in public. He wanted them to understand the permutations and combinations of sound, and to pick up the vibrations from the speaker, that would enable them to detect when someone spoke the truth or told lies. He ensured they learned dancing to understand spatial and body awareness and played a range of melodic and percussive instruments, so that they developed the cultural appreciation that would ensure that Ayodhya would continue to host the best Performing Arts festivals.

Architecture and the environment were also great essentials in Dasaratha's curriculum for the boys. So was astronomy and the study of planets and their positions, to ensure that all rituals for the well-being of the subjects and the prosperity of the kingdom were conducted in accordance with the scriptures. Transportation via roadways was vital to trade, communication and diplomacy. So, they learnt about bullock-cart tolls and tolls for horses and elephants; and that vehicles included chariots, carriages, palanquins and carts. In the surrounding forests, efforts were made to document bird songs and information about wildlife. Any change of patterns unique to each season or climate indicated a change of practice in hunting. They learnt to take measures to ensure the breeding of various species of birds and animals and also to study the causes of extinction, which had an impact on human life as many people kept animals and birds as pets, and indeed hunted them for food. Understanding the seasons and the measure of the harvest, as well as ensuring that gifts were made to loyal subjects appropriately and according to the scriptures at festivals, were deemed important in their education as well.

Dasaratha taught them all this and more . . . and as they grew, he saw that there was a strong bond of affection between Rama and his brothers.

* * *

Well, sixteen years passed and now these young men had grown strong. At that time, to King Dasaratha's court came Sage Viswamithra. Viswamithra was a *brahmarishi*, the greatest of sages of his time. Sages were known to live and work for a hundred and twenty or thirty years. At one time, he had been a warrior king and was known as 'Scorcher of Foes'. Viswamithra longed for immortality. But he realized after many wars that immortality did not come from defeating his enemies or their death. It came from peace. Peace within his restless body, and peace towards nature and people. He gave up his kingship and went to study the nature of peace. Along with some other sages, he set up a hermitage in the Dandaka forest and there, he prayed for the peace and progress of mankind. It was not a passive way of life. It was a dynamic revolution of living in peace by observing behaviour and perceiving the beast in man and compassion among animals. Thus, in the hermitage following a way of studying the mind and how it varies in viewing life under different emotions like fear, or joy, they were able to create a science of the self or yoga by understanding the fine light that makes us

who we are and lives on long after our mortal bodies have
ceased to.

But, in Dandaka, three rakshasa demons, Tataka and
her two sons Subahu and Maricha, were polluting the
forests. They poured oil into the forest streams choking
fish and other water-borne animals. Much of this was done
out of boredom and exercising power through terror. Not
only that, they poured the blood and flesh of animals into
the sages' sacrificial pyres of sacred grass and bark. So,
when Viswamithra walked into the court of Dasaratha, he
had come on a very specific mission—to rid the forests of
this menace. More than that, he wanted to bring about
a renewal of balance in the forces of nature in the forest,
because he knew the earth could heal itself. But the
intervention needed was to bring a human to rid the forest
of terror and, more importantly, to develop a relationship
with the environment. In establishing this, there needed to
be mutual caring between humans and the environment.

Everybody offered him salutations and welcomed
him with sandalwood paste and rose water, but he waved
them aside and went straight to Dasaratha and said, 'I
want your son Rama'. Dasaratha knew what the Dandaka
forest was like.

'Please, why don't you take my armies, chariots and my
best soldiers? All of them are at your command. Rama as
you know is still a young boy,' he pleaded.

Sage Viswamithra could sense the paternal anguish in
Dasaratha. He flinched at this show of sentimentality in a
king. He realized Dasaratha was not yet ready to test his

son for the greater good. 'Why waste time,' he thought, and rose like lightning to leave this court and make other arrangements for the protection of the Dandaka forest. Dasaratha, beleaguered by the sage's request, could not see the consequences of his refusal to send Rama. He had in some way weakened in his word to his people and the earth that the protection of the forests and sages was of high priority. But his chief counsellor, Sage Vashishta, could see what this could mean in terms of the welfare of the state. Letting a great warrior sage like Viswamithra walk away in what seemed like a huff was poor diplomacy and gross discourtesy to intellectualism and the civilized society that Kosala professed to be during Dasaratha's rule. How does one steer the direction of something from tumbling and crashing downwards? Insight and immediate action.

In an instant, Vashishta ran after Viswamithra who was striding past the terrified courtiers. 'Your Lordship, please reconsider as you were a king once too. Those who have anxieties of family . . . they need a little more patience to be dealt with.' Viswamithra stopped. There was a sigh of relief. At least now there could be dialogue, a more peaceful negotiation, rather than a cold war between a powerful sage and a king, with seriously unfavourable consequences throughout the kingdoms that had declared Dasaratha King of Kings.

Viswamithra came forward and looked intently at Dasaratha and said, 'O Dasaratha! When a sapling grows at the root of its parent tree, it gets smothered in its shade, that is why, I tried to pluck Rama from you. I will give him guidance and all the skills. He will grow from my learning as well. After all, the sum of human existence is to grow to one's fullest potential. Rama's learning must be put to the test. This is the perfect opportunity.'

Dasaratha understood. Rama after all was not only his son, he was a prince and had a responsibility to the welfare of others. 'Then take Lakshmana too. They are inseparable,' is all Dasaratha could find himself saying.

Rama and Lakshmana were summoned. Their eyes lit up. What adventures awaited them! Just imagine going with the great Sage Viswamithra. They didn't even know what lay ahead.

And so, before dawn could break in the sky, the next day Viswamithra, Rama and Lakshmana headed for the forests.

They passed through some forests. It was quite uneventful, and then as they came closer to Dandaka, they passed through a deserted landscape. It was like walking into shimmering white heat. Just the thought of putting a bare foot on those sands made the young men quiver. They could see little mounds in the distance. At first, Rama and Lakshmana thought these mounds might offer some shade in this treeless place. But when they looked closer, these were just bleached bones, possibly of travellers, prisoners and desperate animals that were trapped in the desert while attempting to escape from bandits, police or hunters.

But Viswamithra had an *adibala* mantra. He blew a cool tunnel of air and slowly Rama, Lakshmana and the sage waded through its cool stream. At long last they reached Dandaka forest.

There was sunlight a few seconds ago, but in the forest it was pitch dark. The air was rife with the smell of rotten flesh and the river full of dead fish. In the holes below the trees, birds were hiding; snakes were dangling from the branches of trees. And tigers, who should have been roaring, were now mewing like kittens. It was as if nature had turned topsy-turvy. What a strange place this Dandaka forest was! They could hear strange sounds of someone laughing. First, Rama could hear laughter and then he saw an orange tongue of fire slithering through the forest. He knew this was a demon rakshasa in disguise. He arched his arrows in his bow and shot swiftly. The earth split open and the huge cloud of smoke from the slither of fire dissolved.

Where was Lakshmana? Lakshmana was in another part of the forest stalking like a tiger should and as he looked around him, he heard a strange sound. He could not see anything, but soon he began to feel poisonous fumes entering his bloodstream. A strange creature with spiky fur wound itself around him like a python and began to choke him. With his last breath, he managed to gouge an arrow into its head. It struck the eyes of the strange creature which began to wobble and foam. It formed an oil slick and slowly dissolved into the earth as it cleaved open. Two of the worst demons of that time, Tataka and her elder son had been killed. But one of them, Maricha, slipped away into another forest. He was amazed at what Rama and Lakshmana, two ordinary human beings, could do. He decided to hide in another forest and mend his ways. He will come back into our story.

But what of the forest? Suddenly there was a shaft of sunlight that created an arc that stretched like a rainbow across Rama. Then the light created beautiful patterns on the forest floor, as if to bring to life the first touch of colour. Flowers like flames in a forest, orange and yellow, burst open from their buds. The darting turquoise of a kingfisher flew past followed by the shrieking of parrots in their plumes of green and pomegranate pink beaks. Snakes slowly slithered down from trees in broad patterned skins and began to burrow themselves into the forest.

It seemed as if the balance of life had returned to the forests. In the distance, it sounded like music. It was none other than the gurgling of the forest streams. Fish almost turned on their sides and began to swim, the sun shot rainbow arcs on their silver scales. Rama and Lakshmana thanked Viswamithra for having trusted them to accomplish this amazing feat, but he smiled and said, 'There are more adventures in store. But for now, we must leave the forest.'

Kanda II

3

Sita

In Devaloka, Lakshmi's maid continued to wail. Where had Lakshmi vanished to and how? That too, before hearing the verdict from the Greats! Why? The devas and devis tried to calm the maid and tried to understand, between her spluttering, what had really happened.

It so happened that Narada had been cruising across all the planets after his encounter with Ratnakar (who became Valmiki).

The Planet Shani or Saturn was heating rapidly, and its radiation was going to explode into the cosmic dance of the planets. Narada hoped he could divert this negative energy, which could cause aggression and delusions in the human mind. It was evident he would have to call upon the Greats. Having negotiated a safe passage into Space after noting the ascendance of Chandra on the moon, it seemed a good sign to deflect the radiation from Shani. It was evident that

Narada would have to call upon the Greats. He decided to go to Devaloka and tell them of all that was transpiring on and around earth.

It had taken him quite a few years of earth time to disembark at Devaloka. He was space weary. There was hardly any water at the planet stations and even a great soul like Narada, who travelled with the speed of light by the energy of his thoughts, had the necessary afflictions of a human body. He finally arrived in Devaloka at a time when no one was around on the glittering paved pathways. So he decided that he would go to Vishnu and Lakshmi's home known as Vaikuntha. They were by far the most hospitable of the Greats. He always had the privilege of walking into their inner apartments, without a reception line of heavenly messengers in the hallway, as was the case at Brahma's. Vishnu welcomed with heart, and all formalities were done away with.

But when he stepped into the inner courtyard, Narada saw Lakshmi's maid gazing at her loveliness in the water tank at the centre of the courtyard. He called her once, but she was lost in the beauty of Lakshmi's reflection. She had smooth arms, the colour and fragrance of sandalwood. Her lashes rimmed her doe eyes like kohl. Her slender limbs held the weight of her bosom and hips like the stalks of lotus flowers at dawn. She looked so languorous. Narada called again, less sharply, and when their eyes met, she blurted out, 'How dare you!'

'How dare *you*?!' said Narada.

'How dare you walk in like that, calling out for my mistress, looking at me in that way and then . . .? Oh! My god! It's Narada!'

Who can say why Narada did what he did? He cursed the young woman, 'How dare YOU! Mistaking me for some vagabond, you accused me of something so vulgar! I was looking for your mistress to . . . well, wherever she is I hope she vanishes from Devaloka, is born on earth to a poor, ordinary man, far away from the likes of you! That'll teach you a lesson not to be idling all day long!'

There was a choric gasp from the devas and devis. The maid paused for a moment, taking in their reaction, and then began wailing again, 'How could he curse my mistress! She, who is always so gracious in looking after all her attendants . . . why did he not curse me instead . . . Aiyiyooooo! I can't bear this punishment!' Nothing and no one could comfort her. Neither Ganesha's elephant ears flapping (as he kept bees away from settling on the honey laddus he continued scoffing while hearing the woman's grief), nor Saraswati's gentle stroking of her hair, nor the other devas who tried to commiserate her sorrow. Her sorrow was justified. Lakshmi's absence in Devaloka was already being felt. Even the light felt dim and cold. Suddenly, they felt as if the warmth and glow of life had left them.

Down on earth, a holy, but poor, man lived in a little thatched hut on an abandoned field. He used to wake every morning and bathe in a pond and pray to Vishnu.

Many people used to come to sit by him during the day and through his silence, he was able to heal them of their domestic troubles. Vishnu too, saw that this man did not crave anything in life except to help others. 'How would he go about getting his food?' thought Vishnu and decided that instead of the man having to go and seek alms or a job, why not gift him a cow? Not just an ordinary cow, but a holy cow. The man could carry on his work, and whether the cow went out to graze or not, it would give him a limitless supply of milk. The man collected the milk in a pot, and he would sometimes share it with those who came to him for healing. The poor man knew that this could only be Vishnu who had provided him a gift like the cow. So, while thanking Vishnu as he prayed, he suddenly thought of Lakshmi, and hoped that she would be born on earth as someone's daughter.

At that moment, he saw clouds burst in the sky. He could not see him, but it was Ravana storming through the sky in his aerial chariot.

Ravana was on a mission of 'blood collecting' from holy men. This was a game, at first designed for his amusement. The rule was to seek out and spy on people who were considered holy. Then, with beguiling charm, Ravana would take on different disguises to question these people, at a solitary moment, about the nature of 'good'. He had stunningly complex arguments. What was the need to be good? What if we don't want to be? Why do we have to have a sense of judgement? If life was about celebrating, then why were there so many morals to keep us chained like prisoners when we could be free? If one committed wrong and fled the place, who could catch us for the crime? What on earth is a conscience? Why have one if it keeps making you doubt everything you do? Why should one respect women? Aren't they all the same—sisters, wives, daughters, etc.? Why should we look after the disabled or children? Weakness should be put down! Why should the experience of an elder who does not have the strength physically be taken? What do they have to teach us about life but regret?

The way he defeated his opponents with his strong arguments against 'good' in human nature was subtle. He got a buzz from playing this game and winning. Of course, he was always in disguise as the vulnerable contender, so he caught people unawares. But when a few people challenged him about the need to question one's actions and face the responsibility for those actions, it stopped becoming a game. There was no buzz when Ravana wasn't winning. He soon discovered that the way of accounting for his successes was by collecting the blood of anyone who contested him and labelling them 'holy'. The blood was preserved in several pots in his palace.

On one such occasion, while he was lurking around the hut when the man of the holy cow had gone to the pond for his bath and prayers, Ravana found the pot of holy milk and stole it.

Ravana returned triumphant to his palace with the stolen pot. Then he mixed the blood from his other pots into it. Ravana called his wife, Queen Mandodari, to hide the mixture of blood and milk, that had now turned pink, and warned her that it contained poison. Mandodari was a sensitive woman. She knew the game he was playing at first, had now turned into something exceedingly sinister. When Ravana left on yet another mission, she discovered through her secret intelligence services what he had done. She was disgusted with this behaviour. She decided to drink it and kill herself. To her surprise, when she drank it, she became pregnant. Suddenly, she feared that Ravana would accuse her of having the child from another man or rakshasa. So, after the birth of her baby girl, she told Ravana's brother, Vibhishana, about what had happened. Being a kind and unconventional rakshasa, he had the baby girl taken away to the land across the ocean, north-west of Lanka.

Across the ocean, in the kingdom of Mithila, King Janaka was ploughing a field. He saw something glistening in the distance. As he approached, he noticed a crystal cradle that was wedged in the furrows of the earth and found there was a little baby girl in it. She looked so radiant. He held the child close and took her home to his queen. The child was named Sita, as she was found in the furrows of the earth.

All this happened in a flash from the time Lakshmi vanished from Devaloka when Narada cursed the maid. Lakshmi had fulfilled a poor and holy man's prayer that she be born as a human on earth. The devas, viewing this sight from Devaloka, sighed with relief.

Sita was loved dearly by her royal parents who found her in the furrow of a field which King Janaka was ploughing.

His greatness was in doing ordinary tasks as well as ruling a kingdom, and when it came to his spiritual practice, no one could disturb him. He and his wife felt as if a beam of light had touched their lives, by giving them their only child, and so they named this child Sita.

Sita made friends quickly and treated them as equals. She could have a fiery temper, especially if someone was deceitful. The wise ones in the court often said, 'Sita has the essence of Agni,' the God of Fire. But she had a quick wit, a sense of humour that endeared her to everyone and the gift of being able to soothe any sorrow with a lightness of word or touch, without being insensitive or careless. Her nature was fed by fire. She had an unquenchable desire to live and celebrate life in all its hues.

King Janaka had a prosperous kingdom that rivalled Dasaratha's. But it was not as vast as Kosala, which was naturally gifted with three rivers flowing around it, making it extremely fertile. Mithila depended on trade with other kingdoms and knew the significance of strong regional relationships, rather than standing alone. These relationships enabled the citizens of Mithila to feel safe. Security and a healthy economy often make people feel they can take time out for holidays, or spend time planning elaborate rituals, like naming ceremonies for babies, becoming a teenager, or just travelling and enjoying the countryside, apart from life in the court.

Janaka insisted on holidays for three reasons. Firstly, it enabled people who lived and worked at the court to experience the pace of rural life, and secondly, it enabled the courtiers to discover the needs of the villagers in an unofficial capacity. The third reason was that while on holiday, one could plan for the future. For Janaka, holidays helped him think clearly, away from the pressures of a daily schedule of meetings. It was sheer joy being in the company of his wife and daughter and their friends.

Janaka had an orchard with fruit trees at the rear of the holiday palace. He kept a minimum of servants as this enabled him to be himself and prepare, in due course of time, for his *vanaspratha*, or retirement, when he would have to do the daily chores himself.

He too would pray to Shiva with a sincere heart, every day. One afternoon, he noticed a giant iron bow halfway in the earth, standing up to the height of a banana tree! On it was inscribed 'Janaka, a gift of Love—Shiva'. What in heaven's name was the use of a bow, and that too this size, in his vegetable garden when he was on holiday! 'For Pity's sake,' thought Janaka, 'I have no intention, inclination or time to show any neighbouring kingdom how mighty Mithila is!'

As it was hidden amongst the banana trees, he decided to leave it there while he went away and thought about the best way to show his gratitude to Shiva, being careful not to endanger his kingdom in the eyes of Mithila's neighbours, with what an iron bow could signal.

His queen had cooked with her own hands a simple and satisfying meal of daal, rice and three green vegetables dribbled with ghee. Just as Janaka had finished and gone to the inner courtyard to wash his hands and rinse his mouth, he could see straight through the doorway. He saw that Sita was looking up at the bow. She was in one of her clearing-up-the-garden moods. She had her arms akimbo, and her head tilted to fathom the actual size of the bow underground from its height above ground. Then in a flash, Janaka saw his fifteen-year-old Sita lunge for the bow at its widest arc and with both her hands pull it out and fling it! 'Yes! Take that!' she shouted gleefully, dusting her hands matter-of-factly. 'That'll teach you to wedge into the roots of these fruit trees! What a mess this is,' saying this she began levelling the yawning hole in the ground with the rubble around it.

Janaka was awestruck. That was Shiva's bow Sita had just plucked out and chucked like some soft, rotting plant! Throughout his lunch he was calculating how many men he would have to get to dig that bow out of the ground to then heave it onto a chariot and carry it back to Mithila, 'Oh, it doesn't bear thinking!' he said to himself. Then something dawned on him. 'Sita! Even she is not aware of how extraordinary she is!' That beam of light in her eyes, the fire in her soul, were all signs of how blessed he and his wife were to have her as their daughter. He thought it best not to say anything either to his wife or daughter.

Two weeks passed. Spring was in the air, and the bullock horns were painted with vermilion and turmeric, strung with flowers and bells and streamers. It was time to return to the court for the royal festivities for the birth of a new season.

Janaka, his wife and Sita, with Urmilla Sita's adoptive sister and at heart best friend, were returning in the royal chariot. They were often accompanied by the woman storyteller who knew a thing or two about the different villages and towns they passed. Somehow, she always got hold of the latest news, and this was Janaka's best way of keeping up with what had happened while he was away.

A woman storyteller never just reports facts; she has wonderful emotional twists and turns to events. Urmilla and Sita were listening to her latest information about two young men from the Kosala kingdom who had entered Dandaka forest accompanied by Viswamithra. 'Do you know what they saw!' the storyteller's eyes widened as she could see it clearly in her mind's eye. 'They came upon a large, black rock. One of the young men, being curious, as young men are, was examining this strange stone. His toe grazed the base of it. Then suddenly, it burst into a soft flame, and a woman stepped out. Her name was Ahalya. She was so radiant, a real beauty. You know what her name means?' Even without waiting for a response, she continued, 'The one in whom there is no imperfection.'

'I can't even imagine that!' said Urmilla.

'You mean it's even greater than being just perfect?!' asked Sita indignantly.

'Now that's something for you two to live up to,' said the queen with a warm laugh.

'So, what happened then?' asked Janaka, as he wanted to find out about the two young men and who they were while concealing his concern for the safety of his kingdom.

The storyteller continued cheerfully, impervious to these lively interruptions.

'It was long before my mother's, mother's grandmother's great aunt's time, that if any woman was compared to Ahalya's beauty, all the neighbours would "tut, tut". It wasn't just her beauty; it was her nature that was beyond comparison.

She was a caring woman. She loved her husband who was many, many, many years older than her. He was a great thinker of his time. There they both were. In the forest, in a little hermitage. He used to wake early and go off to meditate and she would make the place spotless by the time he returned. When the devas watched over her, they couldn't help wondering what it would be like to be close to her. But Indra, the chieftain of the devas couldn't hold back any longer. He thought of Ahalya, night and day, and day and night. All the courtesans of Devaloka grew ferociously jealous of a woman on earth preoccupying the passion of a Deva, and that too Indra. They taunted him. He found this a good excuse to come down to earth and prove what a powerful Deva he really was; that no one could stand in the way of such striking godliness. But as the Deva holds the thunderbolt and strikes lightning, he decided not to come to earth so dramatically. It would scare everyone off. He knew the only way he could enter the presence of Ahalya was if he took on a convincing disguise. So, he waited for the husband to leave the hermitage. Then, transforming himself into the husband's double, Indra approached Ahalya. They made love. The husband returned to the hermitage as he had left his water jar behind. He saw them in sheer pleasure . . .'

'Then what happened?' asked the queen, genuinely startled by the turn of events in this story.

'When Ahalya's husband appeared, however great a sage or thinker he was thinking on grand things like immortality, the nature of life and death . . .'

'Go on, go on,' urged Janaka.

'He cursed both his wife and Indra. Ahalya was protesting about how she had been deceived, and even as she did so, she turned to stone for many, many, many years. Her husband did put a condition to the everlasting curse. That only a man who could find no darkness in any being, if he touches the stone, her spell would be broken, and she would be free.'

'And such a man entered Dandaka just a few days ago?' asked Sita genuinely amazed.

'Not only that, Your Highness,' said the chariot driver, 'but he has put an end to the terror in the forests by doing away with those wretched rakshasas Tataka and Subahu.'

'Goodness Gracious!' said Janaka. '. . . and you say such a man is on his way?' Sita asked rather thoughtfully.

4

Mithila

It is exhausting to undertake a journey. First, there is the excitement of preparation, and then the actual journey to look forward to. Imagine the adventure of experiencing new smells and tastes, hearing different languages, and watching different customs that range from a 'welcome' to a 'goodbye' in other cultures! Listening to a story is *about* travelling. You start by listening, not knowing who the characters are. By the time you have finished listening, you are familiar with the characters because you have travelled with them. You are there in their time of trouble, laughter, love, anger, despair and happiness. At the end of the story, you come out of it like you have been visiting another country, and something about that story has changed you and the way you look at life. There are so many characters to meet and names to remember; some we instantly like, others we find instantly odious, but learn to tolerate. Then, of course, there are surprises. We have to have strong stomachs because the twists and turns of life are like riding on a roller coaster.

Rama and Lakshmana had eaten soft kala jamun that had stained their fingers and lips a deep purple with its tangy sweetness, and laughing at how each other looked, lay down on the ground to rest. Lakshmana was delighted he had had a battle with a real rakshasa. His eyes were shining with pride for his beloved Rama, who was his hero. As Viswamithra walked with the brothers through the forest, Lakshmana would frequently look over his shoulder hoping something was lurking around so that he could leap into action. Rama was cool. He enjoyed listening to Viswamithra's stories. He felt as if he were entering the very heart of people's lives, in a way he could not at the palace in Kosala, where everyone loved him and only showed their best side to him.

He was puzzled and pleased in turns by Ahalya's story. 'So strange to be a woman,' he thought. She fulfilled her time of punishment, for a mistake that was not of her making, and as there was no forgiveness from her husband, she bore the weight of his curse that shifted her shape into a big black rock, ungiving and unfeeling. Finally, when she was looked upon with compassion, she felt released from the past, and thanking Rama, she left in a cloud of effervescent light.

They walked barefoot through forests and waded across streams and a wide river with steep embankments. They trusted Viswamithra, who would not reveal the next destination, in the stride and pace he set for travelling by foot and stops to rest. Viswamithra made them listen to different birdsongs and watch their migratory patterns, understand the mating season of the fish, and see the harvesting of wheat and paddy. Rama began to see different kinds of fields. Some were lying fallow, while a set adjacent were fertile for farming.

'Even the soil needs a rest to restore its nutrients,' explained Viswamithra.

'We don't do this in Kosala. It makes perfect sense, though,' said Lakshmana, 'to give the soil a rest before sowing it again. If we don't care for the land, who will?'

'Every forest, hill, field, river and mountain is as good as the men who sow and tend to it,' said Viswamithra with a contented sigh, having been rid of the rakshasa. Rama knew these words would ring true to his heart, throughout his life.

In the distance, they could see paths and soon these broadened into paved roads. Viswamithra was now almost sprinting and the young men had to quicken their pace. They entered a city named Mithila. The gateway was ornate, with thick stone held together by sculptures of dancing men and women, elephants and birds. The cornerstones were engraved with a hunting bow and bordered with Kama, the God of Love's arched bow and a spray of arrows.

Rama and Lakshmana quickly looked at each other. Was this a hostile city under the cover of friendship? They swiftly concealed their curiosity and were soon overtaken by this awe-inspiring city. People had no need to lock their doors.

It was safe in Mithila, the kingdom of Janaka. Precious gems such as emerald and sapphire were bought and sold in the street markets. Prosperity abounded and there were no beggars. Those who were disabled were occupied with creating crafts. There was the vibrance of life lived to its fullest in this capital. The traffic of elephants and horses and bullock carts halted as passenger carriers moved swiftly.

It was close to midday and drinking-water carriers began to line the streets. Rama had stopped for a drink and was checking out the time of day by the position of the sun. It made him look up and at the same time, look at a young woman who happened to be playing ball with her friends up on a balcony. She looked down at the ornamental ball that had fallen on the street below by Rama's feet.

One fleeting glance. That's all it took. It was a turning point. Their worlds would never be the same again. Up to that point, each, in their own little universes, was alert to the senses of this world. But as they caught sight of each other, it was like lightning. He was sure and so was she that the other was from another dimension. The transmission of that information to their hearts and brains was as rapid as a shock wave. Rama was sixteen and she was neither older nor far less in age than him. Suddenly, Rama's world was in slow motion. He could see things moving but hear no sound. He heard the street bands the next minute, but the musicians did not seem to touch the ground as they progressed towards the palace. 'Who could she be?' thought Rama. Lakshmana and he had been close friends as brothers. But now, Rama could not get himself to share his thoughts even with his closest friend. What a strange mixture of extreme joy and twisting pain he felt in his heart as he kept remembering her face, eyes and heaving breast.

'These are the most delicious sun-ripened watermelons,' cried Lakshmana as he slurped his way through the red flesh of the crescent-shaped slice. 'Where did you get them?'

Rama was looking at the knife in his hand as if his body was a stranger to what he felt in his soul.

'Heaven . . .' Rama brought himself to say. Lakshmana, who was busy with the oversized slice over his mouth, looked at Rama.

'What? What's the matter, brother? You look pale! Mithila's heat is inhospitable. Come on . . . let's go in the shade.' And so, because of Lakshmana's concern, Rama was persuaded to move from the spot where he had first been stung by love.

Viswamithra was being mobbed by the devout subjects of Mithila. They all wanted the blessings of this great sage. King Janaka was taking him on a personal and informal tour of the various gifts that had been bestowed upon this kingdom. Janaka led Viswamithra into a large, enclosed pavilion. Inside, covered under a quarter of a mile-long stretch of sapphire blue velvet was the giant iron bow. King Janaka sighed, 'I've been very blessed to have the vision of Shiva and this gift.' Viswamithra could read the burden from under the well-concealed sigh of a good-hearted king.

'Speak plainly Janaka, you haven't brought me away in secret to show me a gift that Shiva dropped in the back garden of your holiday resort?'

'I don't mean to be ungrateful,' said Janaka, 'but I can't really figure out whether this giant bow is a bane or a boon. Sita is a real blessing. To ward off the suitors who were coming in great processions to our kingdom since she was thirteen, I decided to announce that anyone who could lift this bow and twang it would be considered a suitable man, and could wed Sita. No one has been able to do so. Now there are rumours that I do not want Sita to be married. What kind of father does that make me? I so want to see her married and happy!'

'Is that why you have arranged this tournament the day after tomorrow?' asked Viswamithra.

'I cannot tell you how much I pray that the man who is mighty enough to lift that bow, is as gentle to our lovely Sita,' said Janaka, moved to tears.

'We shall see. Let us not waste time dwelling over rumours. They are just mists of our own fears. As a father, if your love is true, then you will do everything in your power to see that your daughter gets a husband of exceptional qualities.'

The beating of the drums in the streets began to fill the air. Viswamithra and Janaka could not complete their private tour, as it was time for the king to conduct his judicial affairs of the day.

As Rama and Lakshmana were returning to their rest house, they noticed people bustling around, creating *mandapams*, or pavilions, and encircling them with pearls. Food was being carried in cartloads to the royal kitchen. The sweet smell of cooked plantains hung in the air. The sun began to set and Viswamithra took the brothers to bathe and meditate by the pond outside the city. It was cow dust hour, and as the cattle were returning home, the vermilion sun was descending in the western sky. The fragrance of night-time flowers intermingled with sandalwood paste that was used for the prayers. The bells of the little shrines of goddesses outside the city gates were chiming, and as night descended, the flames from temple lamps in the distance winked and danced in the blackness.

Rama was silent. What of the young woman who had seen Rama?

5

The Tournament

Sita was no longer the audacious and cheerful playmate Urmilla had known over the holidays, or indeed till this afternoon. What had happened that had changed her so?

If the room was dark, Sita complained it was too cold. When the moon came out, she complained it was too bright and hot. When she lay on her cushioned bed, she grumbled it was too hard. She kept moaning softly and breathing irregularly. Urmilla heard her crying out about how her heart was a captive. 'Who is he?' Sita would suddenly gather the strength to say. 'How dare anyone rob me of my senses when I was awake! He wasn't one of us. Then who was he? Who is the man who has stolen my heart!'

The day passed.

Rama could hardly sleep and woke up early to go to the river to bathe and catch the early morning landscape as it unfurled with the rising sun. It alerted his mind to the sight, sounds and smells of nature before the cityscape would fold him in its human embrace. In his heart, he still felt the longing that had struck him the day before when he gazed into the eyes of that young woman. He had to cast away all thoughts of this. After all, he was a prince, and although he did not know what mission Viswamithra had set for him today, he knew he must focus on being attentive. Lakshmana joined him by the riverbank, and silently they swam, drawing quiet courage from each other before facing a day, whose events were unknown to them. They always waited for Viswamithra to spin them a surprise mission, and found that the reward was in accomplishing it in newfound ways.

Today, Viswamithra was silent. It was a new method, they thought. He blessed them and signalled they follow him. But where? As they left the small village that skirted the city, they saw elephants and camels and town criers cheering and dancing, and many new visitors going to the city. Neither knew about the tournament at Mithila.

The city was festooned with banners carried by the entourage of many princes. Each banner was embossed with the princes' guardian deity; some bore the lion, some had the eagle, some the owl, another the cobra, yet another the peacock and on and on it went as the procession of the entourages was more than a mile long.

Each entourage consisted of the princes' poets, masseurs, astrologists, musicians, councillors, palmists, poison detectives, historians, ateliers, sartorial advisors, and accompanying brahmins, who would invoke their respective gods of strength to win the tournament. The people of Mithila had swept and washed its roads till they gleamed in the sun. There were sugarcane juicers offering clay cups of fresh juice as a welcome drink. Water carriers stood along the roadside, ready to offer refreshments to any member of the entourage. There were elephant sheds and stables provided for each visiting kingdom. Food, drink and diverse entertainments were provided by the royal courtesy of Mithila. Possibly at any other tournament, a prince's entourage could stir a little trouble by drinking too much, losing at gambling or the cockfight, or because a dancing girl slapped them too hard. But here, on this occasion, the tournament and where it was being held had a special significance.

It was Mithila, a coveted city within a coveted kingdom. The princes had been waiting eagerly for the announcement of this tournament for months, even a year. They had been training for longer. Each prince wanted to exhibit his skills and show his prowess. Nothing and nobody could cast a slur on that one ambition that each prince came with, to Mithila. But why?

Because each prince dreamed of winning the prize of the tournament. The prize was Sita. Sita's wit and fiery spirit caught the attention of poets and praise of singers when they attended the arts festivals at Mithila. They, in turn, created legends about her and when they returned to their courts and sang, each prince grew to love Sita and wanted to have her for his wife. Except of course Rama, who had no idea about any of this.

The whole of Mithila was bustling with guests and the streets hummed with languages of other kingdoms. Its kitchens were steaming with cuisines for vegetarians, vegans and meat eaters. Sweet stalls were dressed with sweets of all colours and shapes glistening with silver trim, and the air filled with the subtle aromas of green cardamom, clove, and nutmeg combined with saffron in sweetened, thickened cow's milk. Weavers produced bales of rich turquoise and ruby-coloured silk. The stonecutters' chisels and hammers created early morning music as they carved in soapstone and alabaster, statuettes of women in various forms of movement, subliminally celebrating the vivacity of their princess Sita, without disclosing her identity.

Viswamithra glided past the crowds with his able adjutants. Rama and Lakshmana wore their hair long and tied in a topknot, a practical choice for Viswamithra's apprentices, who travelled through difficult terrain where grooming could be time-consuming. They wore dhotis made of bark and carried a quiver of arrows slung on their backs. Their torsos were bare, and they could well have been mistaken for forest folk. Other princes could not sneer at them as they both had a stately presence; these were cultured and strong young men. To undermine their dignity would only reflect on the crassness of the instigator. The eligibility to the tournament was on democratic grounds; anyone who had training and was recommended by an accredited Brahmin or sportsman was welcomed. Rama and Lakshmana, although unknown in Mithila, and unregistered for the tournament were qualified being

Viswamithra's assistants and were welcomed in the Mithila assembly hall.

It was vast. A huge gong sounded and the waves of sound filled the city. First, the conch shell, a symbol of Vishnu, as a presence that inhabits sound and space, blew. Everyone—princes, entourages, courtiers and invited commoners of Mithila—was hushed. Then the liveried trumpeters announced the powerful ministers of Mithila's court, then the brahmins, then the sages, and finally King Janaka.

Another gong with several chimes sounded and a gold embossed screen that seemed like a wall, folded open. When it opened, a golden chariot covered with a sapphire blue velvet drape emerged. The chariot, guided by eight hundred footmen, rolled forward. It had been timed perfectly; swift enough not to bore the spectators, and steady enough so that everyone marvelled at the feat of sliding in a mile-long chariot into the even larger assembly hall. Another flourish of string and percussion instruments, and trapeze artists flew in from their perches at the corners of the ceiling. With bows like Kama's, they shot hooked arrows at the edges of the drape and pulled it up in unison while performing a fly-past dance. Everyone's mouth popped open, gasping at this synchronized entertainment. There was thunderous applause when the drape was carried away, revealing Shiva's giant iron bow.

The sound filtered up the tower where Sita was, still struck by the look in 'that man's eyes'. 'What!' she sat up startled from her slumber. Looking down at herself, she discovered she had been dressed in a red and gold sari. Her wrists were heavy with gold bangles that belonged to the Queen Mother and her ancestors. On her breast lay the crest jewel of the kingdom. 'What! Is it the festival of the monsoon?! Have the rains started already? Did they let the parrots out?' Urmilla fixed her gaze on her friend and spoke calmly and firmly, 'Darling Sita, today is the tournament. Your father has waited years for this occasion. All the arrangements were made last year. The honour of Mithila rests on you!'

'Oh! How can I explain how my heart rises with the thought of him . . . And how it sinks when I think of those muscle-bound, metal-eating men down there thinking they can lift Shiva's bow! They must be idiots if they think they can . . . Urmilla, don't turn away! You know they'd never be able to do it in a million years!'

'I know Sita but think of your dear father! You, he, and I know that it is impossible to win your hand. But the princes must feel they have had a fair crack at the whip. You have to present yourself when they lose. Now gather yourself. Please!'

'Oh! Nonsense! If I go there in the condition that my heart is in, they will say I am gloating and aloof. Why should I go at all! Why can't I be left in peace to gently let him fade from my heart, just as he so cruelly struck me without any intention of staying!"

Down below, the tournament was beginning. Four hundred and ninety-eight princes had decided to compete. It seemed an odd number. But one among them, Ravana, had registered for two places, as his entourage was twice as large as any other prince, and he really wanted to have two attempts at winning Sita. The great sages, who can see beyond the physical body that we have, would often draw him in their scrolls with ten resplendent heads and twenty arms. He was very accomplished but his vanity and ego got the better of him, time after time. Hence, the depiction of him with multiple heads and arms, always reached beyond himself to fulfil his greed.

Viswamithra stood by the sidelines with Rama and Lakshmana beside him. The first prince was announced. He was preceded by his praise singer who chanted melodically, and rather pompously, of the great ancestors of the prince and how worthy he was. The prince then proceeded to climb five steps up to a platform where the entire gathering could see him. For the people in the city streets, a poet from within the court stood on a stone above a secret passage that channelled the sound of what he recited. These proceedings were heard by the town crier, standing at the end of the secret passage and facing the street, who reported the proceedings for the whole of the city and its visitors to hear.

As each prince came forward, some with braided hair, others with topiary-shaved sideburns, some with waxed whiskers embroidered with precious gems, others with bejewelled tattoos, they all wanted the chronicles to record that in their youth they had attempted to win Sita by trying to lift that impossible bow. Having had the chance, each one of them returned, collapsing into the arms of their masseurs like tents in a thunderstorm, with broken arms and hearts.

Ravana went forward. He who had killed the serpent that frightened the gods, now had his turn. The teeth of many princes chattered and bones rattled as, with each step that Ravana took towards the platform, the earth trembled. Viswamithra sighed. Ravana twirled his moustache. He was the only contestant who competed with his crown on, and his jewels intact. He stood with his left foot held apart and on a higher step from the right foot. A stance that communicated his authority as a wrestler and projected him as indefatigable. He slapped his right thigh. Smack! It resounded in the assembly hall like a thunderclap. He bent down to touch the bow. It felt like running water, so light on his fingers. But when he tried to get a grip, it felt like the weight of the universe was pulling him into the ground. His masseurs deceitfully tried to anchor his feet to the ground so he would not slip, but Ravana snarled with viciousness and vowed to break their legs.

Each contestant was set a time for the attempt at lifting the bow. Ravana had been distracted by the masseurs and his reaction to them. Second attempt. He stretched his arms into the air and lunged to pick up the bow. The blood rushed to his head, he let out the grunt. The wail of weightlifters as he tried to lift the bow, the gong, linked to the channel of water that measured the time, chimed, automatically setting off prisms of light so every contestant had to stop. Phew! Ravana was almost relieved this ordeal was over. He would not, indeed he could not, lift that bow. Majestically, sneering at the timekeepers, he covered the wounds of his broken heart with a scornful smile that indicated the tournament was not sophisticated enough for the likes of him.

He strode out of the assembly hall with his attendants, with what everyone else read as contempt. There was an uneasy silence. This was followed by the final, or 500th contestant (remember, Ravana had taken two turns at lifting the bow, so there was one place short to make up five hundred). He was a wiry fellow with a dismissive manner that could reduce anything to nothing with his cynicism. When he saw that Ravana was defeated by the task, he knew what his fate would be. He would never be able to lift that Shiva bow in this lifetime or any other. He had never accepted humiliation and had only come to socialize at the tournament, so he decided on a new tactic.

'Friends!' he proclaimed to the thousands in the assembly hall as well as those outside, 'this tournament is a hoax!' There was a chorus of gasps followed by muttering. Janaka, in his wisdom, remained seated. Had he stood up, the guards would have taken that as a signal that the security of the kingdom was under threat. Janaka, advised by his ministers and sages, wanted to hear the claims of this contestant. 'You hear me? WE, all of you and I, have been cheated. We have been seduced by the glamorous hospitality of Mithila. Our senses have been dulled. What has really happened is that we have been tricked into believing that any one of us could actually lift Shiva's bow. King Janaka does not wish to marry away his daughter Sita, so he has made us look like fools, while he will gain the status of King of Kings and his daughter!"

A storm of mutterings, gasps and grunts filled the assembly hall. Those who were horrified, mostly the courtiers of Mithila and its neighbouring allies, gasped and grunted at these accusations. But there were mutterings of agreement from some of the demoralized princes and their entourages, who were relieved that someone had the courage to say what they were too cowardly to express. At the word 'cheated', there was a great release of frustration and a chorus of approval from that quarter. The wiry prince gained confidence. He had supporters. He realized it was only a matter of language to turn the tide of popularity in his favour. So he cried, 'How do we know, my brothers and friends, those of you who believe what I say, and those of you who cannot peel the scales from your eyes, how do you know that at this very moment, the gateways to your kingdoms are safe from the rampaging armies of Mithila? Can we guarantee that our mothers, sisters, daughters, and the brides and wives of our subjects are not being attacked while we are being held hostage with this hospitality?'

A twinge in the right calf muscle, caused by an old injury, made Janaka stand up with a start, and this of course signalled a contradictory message. The wiry prince was quick and with a clenched fist, he raised his arm and cried 'WAR!' There were hundreds of fists rising in the assembly hall, the rings on their fingers glinting like flames from torches that would spread like a forest fire. The cry was unanimous: '*War!*' In one nanosecond, the tide of celebration and festivity had turned into hostility that could lead to destruction.

'That's all an atom of thought takes to explode—a nanosecond', thought Viswamithra as he watched. 'Amazing how the human reaction can swing from one extreme to another, and how one egoistic person can seize the moment, like a chimpanzee banging a drum, and change the tide of human history for worse. I must do something now.'

Viswamithra was tall, and even though he stood at the side, he was visible from all sides of the assembly hall. He was quick as a flash. In that one split second when all eyes and mouths were shouting 'War' in the direction of where Janaka was standing, Viswamithra too raised his arm, but his palm was open, facing the angry crowds.

It was customary that when the archbishop of sages such as Viswamithra made a gesture, everyone took notice and the sheer authority of his being, reduced people from shouting to mumbling. Then there was a hush. Rama was summoned. All this was signalled by Viswamithra's eyes. No words were spoken. Rama was a young man, with hardly any hair on his chest. He had no entourage of praise singers or masseurs to give him moral and physical support. He had no idea this tournament led to a prize that was a lifelong commitment. He believed he was on a specific mission with his guru, and that he must focus on the task at hand. He was focusing on his breath, the moment that made him conscious of life. Lakshmana's eyes followed his brother's back, standing tall, breathing deep yet calm. Both brothers carried the lineage of the Ishvaku. Leaving aside claims of royalty, their thoughts had merged with the teaching that Vishwamithra had instructed; single-mindedness in the task set before them. In Dandaka forest, despite the shape-shifting distractions of the rakshasas, Rama realized that the test of single-mindedness is focus and dedication to something greater than him. He couldn't understand it but it was as if the life of all plants and animals, the earth herself, was calling out to him for protection. If he did not rise to this call, suddenly he feared everything would face extinction. By focusing on the mission of returning life to the forest, Rama overcame the sinking feeling of fear by finding strength in breathing and visualizing a soft and bright flame of light within him. It was a daily practice. The only intention of the rakshasas was to destroy. Vishwamitra had subtly taught Rama that what matters most is life in the forests. It sustains life for humans too.

In Mithila's Assembly Hall, the atmosphere was filled with human anticipation. For Rama, was it the bow of Shiva he saw? Or was it a mighty instrument and a challenge that had been placed before him? Lakshmana wondered what Rama was looking at for so long. Was he working out how to do it? His expression was that of the cool moonlight that sheds its rays on everything with a soft clarity. Some wondered, who were these forest men who dared attempt to enter the tournament. These were just arrows of thoughts in peoples' heads. Every being was silent, waiting, watching.

Everyone was mesmerized by his litheness. But they were also convinced that they were going to witness an act of gross misjudgement and decided to hold Viswamithra responsible for the consequences of a brave and beautiful warrior ending up as dead as a dung cake.

Rama closed his eyes and uttered a mantra quietly that led him to the eternal sound of the murmuring bee within him as it created a powerful vibration of energy. He then bent down and touched the base of the bow with his head.

Everyone gasped as he lifted the bow on its side, his fingertips slid down the length of the bowstring and up again. The incredible and subtle power of his fingertips made the bow of Shiva crack in two! It was unbelievable. The musicians instantly expressed joy and began to play of their own accord. The dancers spun. The courtiers forgot their puffy manners and began clapping rhythmically into an ovation.

At that moment, Sita came spiralling down a jasmine-bedecked sandalwood stairway. She had heard the bow snap and was curious to see who had managed the feat. 'That's him! The man who stole my heart yesterday!' she exclaimed to herself. She was now trembling with relief that she was going to be marrying him. This man whose name was on everyone's lips. 'Rama!' She willingly inscribed it in her heart, that very name: Rama, whispered with every breath, whether waking or asleep. It shook the very earth beneath her feet.

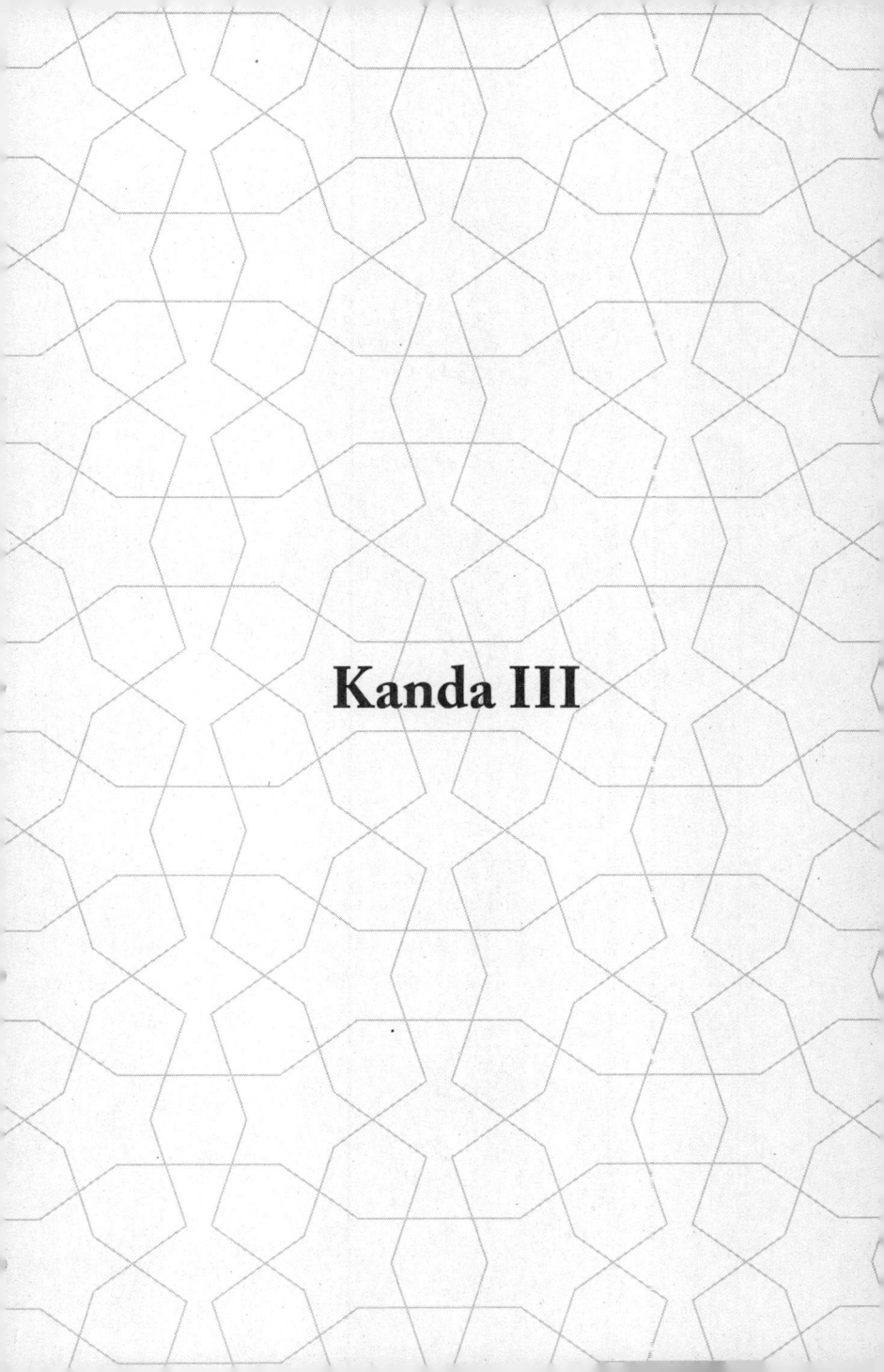

Kanda III

6

Marrying Heaven and Earth

The scent of rose, kannakambaram and tulasi leaves filled the air as a soft haze of their petals floated from the heavens to make a rainbow bridge to earth. Conch shells were blown, cymbals were struck, elephants trumpeted, and crowds cheered and sang with such abandon. In one moment, they could have been victims ravaged by war, but instead, by the flick of an open palm, they were now celebrating a rite of passage. Janaka wept with joy. Even the 498 disgruntled princes felt they had to join in, as now Sita, not just her legend, was standing there in front of Rama, completely enthralled by him, as Rama was by her.

A black stone was placed at Sita's feet, and she placed her left foot on it. Rama knelt down and placed a ring on her second toe, taking his vows to hold her life in greater esteem than his own. Their eyes met, suffusing his heart with light. For the first time, his lips and fingers trembled.

This was the gaze that had stolen his heart a couple of days ago. He had first set eyes on her, up on the balcony, and when after looking at him, she turned away, it had left him feeling that if he were never to see her again it was best he was dead. But for the fact that his family loved him, and his own balanced temperament that reminded him he was a successor of dynasties of kings, he was ready to kill himself.

As her steady gaze held his, his heart fluttered. Her eyes, in turn, were captivated by the spell of his head rising above hers. Now, he could see the white moons of her eyes as she looked up at him. Both their heads were light atop their spines, buoying in an ocean of joy. 'How could one,' he thought, 'feel so grounded, and yet have the earth give way under the feet all at once?'

'This must be love,' she thought.

'How can one feel the happiness of sorrow leaving, and at the same time feel sorrow, worrying that the happiness may be momentary?' he thought.

'I have bound my loneliness to this companion, and he has bound his loneliness to my companionship so that we can always be one,' she thought.

She raised her arms to place the garland of jasmine flowers over her beloved, the true victor of the torment of her heart, the one who brought victory to all those who loved peace. The tips of her fingers accidentally grazed past his left temple, making the hair on his neck stand on end. His lips caught the base of her palm as her hands journeyed back to her sides and the sudden beads of perspiration on her brow winked like diamonds. He placed the garland with such lightness around her head, so that her hair, jewellery, or sari was neither weighed down nor entangled in the jasmine.

The brahmins chanted and the fire altar blazed. The flames rose, crackling and lisping, as Rama recited the *Mangalasutra mantram*: 'My Beloved! O auspicious one! I tie this mangalasutra around your neck. You are the reason for me to live. May you live a hundred autumns!'*

The end of Sita's sari was tied to an *angavastram*, a long cloth that had been placed around Rama's neck. She started the *saptapadi* (a cycle of seven vows around the altar fire), left foot first, and Rama followed. Sita began: 'All your wealth and grains you shall place under my charge and shall hereafter honour and respect me.' And Rama followed: 'It shall be so. Let us take this step in the first cycle together, towards food and the necessities of life.'

Each cycle was dedicated to an aspect of befriending, caring, and honouring each other across the four stages or ashramas of life. The first was the stage of learning and acquiring knowledge, known as the *brahmacharya* ashrama.

The second, that they had now entered was the *grihasthya* ashrama of marriage was that of being householders. It wasn't just about the two of them. It was about how householders were the nucleus of a well-balanced society, by giving alms, feeding the poor and the workers, sheltering the destitute, raising children with sensitivity, maintaining

---

* *Mangalyatantunanena mama jivanahetuna*
  Kante badhnami subhage tvam jiva saradam satam

the rites of passage with prescribed rituals, celebrating festivals to propitiate the elements who were worshipped as gods and goddesses within the six seasons, providing for their families and caring for the sick and the elderly. In their time of leisure, married couples were encouraged to refine the self by participating in the arts, and also constantly remembering the timeless and universal values in life. This was achieved through devotion to a personal god, symbolizing love and by practising a spiritual and religious discipline known as Bhakti yoga. This presence in every creature, be it human or animal, and throughout nature, was what sustained life on earth. The name given to that faith was Vishnu, believed by followers to be the essence that manifested itself in many incarnations across time, during the evolution of the species from fish to man. These manifestations of Vishnu were the Dasavatara.

In the *Vanaprastha* ashrama, the third stage, they had to consider the marriage of their children while looking towards handing responsibility over to the next generation, and then preparing for the fourth ashrama.

Sanyasa ashrama was the final stage, when the couple devotes their entire time to renouncing all possessions, mentally at first, while contemplating the soul for peace and light through a renewed practice of meditation known as *japa* and *dhyana*. It was believed that if the body had lived a complete life, fulfilling all desires, then instead of accumulating more desires about property, or possessive feelings over a spouse, children or friends, it would be ready to depart the mortal world without a struggle at the time of death, so the soul could finally return to what was considered god: Vishnu, pure light, the ultimate truth. A fantastic theory for some, but for the wise ones who had embraced it, this way of life harmonized well with the stages of youth, ageing, maturity and preparation for death. At least it offered a sense of direction and a code of practice. This code of practice became law. The law of life known as Dharma originating from the Vedas. It depended on the ruler of the land to execute this code of law justly. Otherwise, there would be natural disorder and corruption would take over. That's why it had to be an oath that was sworn in at a marriage ceremony, on whose foundation harmony rests.

In the sixth cycle, Sita said: 'Wherever you are, there I shall be. Beloved, do not transgress me, nor shall I ever transgress you. In your religious rites and acts of charity, I shall be with you, your companion in spiritual pursuits, in material means and in passionate desires.' She had uttered the secret inscribed in her heart in public. Rama replied: 'May it be so. Let us take this sixth cycle towards six good seasons throughout all the years of life.' With the seventh cycle, they had proclaimed their vows as truthful promises to the elements, and the public that was their witness. These vows were not solely for the enjoyment of their own lives, but for creating patterns of harmony that would multiply in their lives and in the lives of all those they touched—the individual and the social nucleus.

For Rama, it was a particular shift from how marriage existed in Ayodhya, where men could take as many wives as they could. His father Dasaratha had three wives, each of whom Rama was taught to respect as his biological mother. In his own marriage, however, Rama decided Sita would be his only wife, his only lifelong companion.

Although the other princes had lost the tournament, they couldn't help but shower good wishes on this simple and radiant couple who were taking their vows. For the courtiers of Mithila, their beloved Sita was a goddess on earth and the jubilation out in the streets was an apt celebration.

But while Rama and Sita's wedding was taking place, beside their altar, another one was set, as Janaka, guided by Viswamithra who saw this as the moment for Urmilla to wed Lakshmana. In this way, neither bride from Mithila would feel homesick in their father-in-law's home in Ayodhya.

Everything seemed to be swimming around Sita. She had barely begun to recover from the heart broken by the encounter the day before when it was suddenly made whole again. Before she could feel the pain of parting from her childhood home, Janaka had seen to it that her dearest friend Urmilla would be beside her. Lakshmana valiantly placed the ring on Urmilla's toe, as he gazed at Rama. Urmilla knew she had found a husband who would always be devoted to Rama, just as she would always be a friend to Sita.

Once the mangalasutras or bonds of marriage were tied around the Mithila princess and her favourite companion by the princes of Ayodhya, Janaka and his ministers knew this would be a sound political allegiance between the two kingdoms. There would be constant traffic between them as gifts from the brides' kingdom would be frequent in the first year. Not only the ministers, but merchants as well were having similar thoughts. If the gifts to Ayodhya were products crafted in Mithila—be it jewellery, boats, carts, utensils, furniture or precious stones—or indeed produce from Mithila, this would be an ideal opportunity to promote trade between the two capitals. Ayodhya being the oldest kingdom and Dasaratha just having been crowned King of Kings, Mithila would always be safeguarded from being invaded, or fighting a war, as it had such a powerful ally. So, from being witness to the stunning spectacle of Ram and Sita's wedding, many of the courtiers saw this as the dawning of a new era in economic expansion, military security through diplomatic negotiation, and tourism, to name a few advantages to this happy union.

Rama and Sita, Urmilla and Lakshmana took their marriage vows before the fire, Agni, who is the judge of purity because it reduces every living thing on earth to its fundamental building block of carbon. Everything, high or low, big or small, when tested by Agni, turns to ash. It was believed that Agni was the only chord of communication between heaven and earth and was, thus, worshipped as sacred.

Then the time arrived to receive the *aashirvadam* or blessings of everyone. So the couples were escorted along the high-carved pillars of the assembly hall with all the princes, their entourages, and the ministers and courtiers showering them with petals and saffron-coloured rice, and into the grand pavilion on the street at the end of the road.

At last, all the visiting crowds from other kingdoms and the workers of Mithila could see the reason for the rapturous cheers they could hear coming out of the assembly hall. Out in the open, the spirit of cheer was freer. Under the sun, the multitude of people from different tribes, villages and professions, came with their heartfelt affection and offered gifts that they could barely afford. But the love they showed for Sita was overwhelming. They also welcomed her 'choice' of husband. Rama was welcomed as a son-in-law, or brother-in-law, as Sita was considered everyone's daughter or sister. These greetings were as much a reflection of the trust they vested in King Janaka. If this was an election, then Janaka would be premier till his life ended, and undoubtedly Sita would take over after him!

Bulls with painted horns and streamers marking the beginning of spring strutted before the royal couple. This was the first time that spring was greeted with clouds of coloured powder as part of the tournament ceremony. There were clay pots with lassi, sweetened with sugar cane juice, or salted and dusted with cumin, supplied in abundance for everyone dancing in the sun. It was possible that *bhang* and opium weren't selling very well that day, because everyone, even the tobacconist and layabout, was intoxicated by the sight of Sita and Urmilla beaming with delight, having married two down-to-earth young men who were willing to walk the streets of the common person. That was what was princely about them. Rama and Lakshmana had no entourage but engaged with the people of Mithila with respect and a ready sense of jolliness.

There were dancers who created the eight stages of marriage in their dance in a large circle that encompassed Rama and Sita. It included the honeymoon, domestic quarrels, rites of passage, staged with raucous humour at times, and the delicate negotiation that was needed in living with one another. Much of this entertainment was delivered with the pride of a people who were 'giving their daughter' away. So Rama had to learn what it meant to marry into another family, leave all your friends, associates and childhood memories, to go and live in a distant land. He understood even more how much he would care for her, particularly her feelings. As he gently led her up the steps to sit on the platform for yet another session of entertainment, he gently squeezed her hand.

Even tribals from neighbouring forests joined in, distinguished by their unique tattoos and animal skins with rattling bone and dried gourds creating a melodic percussion. Then the singing parrots, with their ruby red collars and beaks, were let out, their flight spraying the skyline with arrows of green. Sita was taking in all the sights, and the only music that she could hear from the singing parrots was:

Hail to the king of hearts,
born of moonlit midnight's hue,
two syllables capture his name, Ra Ma! Ra Ma!
Keep repeating and illusions will fall away from the Truth!

She gave a fulfilled sigh and as she gazed after them, Rama caught her eye and edged closer to her. Smiling, they were both enchanted by the excellent display of art and the devotion of Mithila's people to their beloved princess. Rama knew that to have received this kind of love from one's people, one would have had to endear oneself to people in a way that only Sita could, meeting them and hearing their concerns and then representing them to the respective ministers at court, and to the king.

An ensemble of metal percussion and wind instruments marched past. Then, there was a rumble of growing applause as the crowd looked up at the sky.

Sita looked up and gleefully said to Rama: 'This is Mithila's best-kept secret. The Kite festival!' He shielded his eyes from the bright sun and as he looked up, he saw gigantic kites made from the pith of the banana trunk, skilfully creating a puppet drama in the sky. It was a story of two birds in the breeding season. Brightly plumed in yellow and green, the female was attracted by the male. A spirited dance ensued in the sky, with the brightly coloured kite puppets, spanning some sixty feet wide by ninety feet tall, playing the roles of the birds, while the music accompanied them from the earth below. The female bird at first does not want to have just a good-looking companion, but someone who is going to give her a family, sang the narrators in the band. The female finally agrees to accept the male as she would like to have a strong brood of birds. Just as the dance of courtship begins, another giant kite puppet in the form of a hunter appears. The crowds from below boo and hiss him away. The dance of the love birds gathers pace. The crowds cheer and clap. Dark clouds of monsoon started floating their way into Mithila. The music became fast and furious. Suddenly, an arrow-shaped kite puppet shoots up from behind the royal mango grove and strikes the male kite puppet in the chest, the action accompanied by a clash of cymbals. Yards of vermilion-coloured cloth flow out of the male puppet kite. The female puppet kite is still whirling in the dance of courtship. The *nadasaram* from the band screeches, as the female puppet kite sees with horror, her lover dying.

The crowds heckle, threatening to kill the puppeteer for writing such a tragic plot on such a happy occasion. While the *Sutradhara* of the sky puppet show was calming the crowds, the show continued. Sita gasped at the male puppet falling, his chest cut in half. Rama put his arm around her shoulder, even as he flinched at the female puppet's lament of losing her love at a time of pleasure, sung so soulfully by the narrators of the band. The crowds now watched colourful trails in the sky as the hunter puppet approached and began accusing him. With the backdrop of the dark rain clouds, fireworks were set off and against their light, the hunter revealed himself as a god who was testing the sincerity of the female puppet, and being pleased, rewarded her with the life of her dying mate. More fireworks were released. Some cheered, some felt disgruntled by the hasty ending, others justified the viewing by commenting that if something inauspicious is seen, then it takes away the evil eye from so much unmitigated happiness and should be thought of as a blessing.

While Sita and Rama were recovering from the shock of the larger-than-life puppet show, the fireworks made them jump. They laughed at their silly fears.

More dark clouds blocked the clear sky. The breeze drifted the scent of the budding mango flowers. Thunder rumbled.

Valmiki the storyteller was still dreaming this poem called Ramayana. He could sit in the past while looking into the future. He looked at Rama and Sita's face with his inner eye and shared their happiness. But dark clouds were rising in his heart. He knew too well that in the wheel of life, joy is followed by sorrow. He looked again into the future.

The crowds at Mithila were now singing as the elephants came in a long parade and bowed down to the married couples. The conch shells blew, the lead elephant trumpeted and the long drums began their mesmeric beat.

Only one person left Mithila, brooding. Seeing Sita's happiness filled his heart with so many different feelings. He understood her happiness because he loved her so much. But he had wanted to be the object of that happiness. Because there was someone else who took that away from him, his heart twisted in pain. He felt crumpled. He strode into his chariot, and as it raised clouds of dust, no one noticed. The first drops of rain began to fall. Everyone in Mithila said this was a blessing. But Ravana hissed, and bit his tongue as he cried, riding as far away from this scene of happiness as possible.

7

Tall Dreams, Short Straw

Back at Ayodhya, people were going about their business with a sense of mundane eventuality. The sports and dance and music events went smoothly enough, but people quietly complained that there just wasn't any spark to it. Some even dared to suggest that things were so prosperous at Ayodhya that people did not know its value, and suggested that if a false threat of war from a neighbouring kingdom was created, it just might stir some adrenaline. Just the thought was alarming enough. The one who dared express such a thing was strongly advised to banish the thought before rumour got to King Dasaratha.

The real problem in Ayodhya was that everyone was bored. Rama and Lakshmana had gone away on an adventure. Dasaratha would have liked to have sent a few escorts, or even spies, just to ensure that they were safe and had a regular report of their welfare. But that would have insulted Sage Viswamithra. So, there was no news about them. Everyone feared the worst, hoped for the best and had to carry on with life as normal, even though there was no joy in it. Even Bharatha and Shatrughuna, after recovering from the hurt of being left behind, the four brothers never having been separated in all their sixteen years together, felt listless.

Nearly two months had passed. The Indian winter had turned to spring, and the cattle breeding ceremony had arrived. Handsome hump bulls ornamented with brightly plumed silver caps to their horns, saddles embroidered with winking mirrors, and brass bells around their necks and on their hooves came to the Sarayu River in a taurine strut that must have made them very eligible. The cows, with their thick lashes and large black eyes, stood diminutively in the water, taking a dip in the river. The cowboys would seek a proper mate for their cow by testing the bull's tail to see that it did not buck. The cows were picked by their sturdiness and the duration of their breeding season.

While all the bargaining and negotiating was in full swing for the best deal in breeding, a horseman from Mithila rode past. People only noticed him because the horse was not the sturdy kind they were used to in Ayodhya. He did not have their customary martial bearing. There was a lightness to him, and they marvelled at his speed.

Within the hour, the trumpeters were summoning crowds from their ritual by the river to the central market. Everybody was keen to know what news the messenger brought with him. When the town crier announced that Prince Rama was married, there was a pause. A nanosecond of silence. And then, there were sniffles, even tears! What an anticlimax for the messenger who had come from Mithila, who had seen nothing but dust clouds being raised under the stamping feet of celebration dances, open mouths brimming with laughter in his beloved home country. He happened to ask the councillor next to him, who muttered solemnly: 'But why didn't Rama tell *us* first? Why were we not the first to know about this? And where is he? Or has he already been claimed by his wife? He *can't* be henpecked already!'

The messenger couldn't resist tapping the town crier to suggest he had something to say and requested it be translated into the Ayodhya dialect.

'Good people of Ayodhya!' the messenger from Mithila began, 'I bring a heart blossoming with this season's greetings. May your cattle be strong and offer you health and prosperity, and the rains for the harvest make the wealth of your kingdom glorious, and long may your kin be led by the greatness of your powerful King Dasaratha. Our people of Mithila are overjoyed that Prince Rama has wed our Princess Sita, and now accompanied by Sage Viswamithra and followed by Prince Lakshmana and his bride Urmilla, are travelling and will arrive before night falls in Ayodhya.'

That was about nine hours from now! That's no time at all chorused the crowd. What, no time to prepare?! What did one start with first? People were swarming against each other the way bees do when disturbed from their hive. In groups, the various professionals of Ayodhya started pulling at straws. Whoever pulled the shortest straw would have to be the last department to start the task of getting the city ready for the welcome as they would have to offer their resources, human and financial, to other departments to get going with great speed.

So, in a trice, like some great magician was at work, illusion after illusion was created. What looked like a stack of bamboo now became a pavilion bedecked with mango leaves and banana stalks. From the deep interiors of the palace temple, lamps were brought out. Clay pots were filled with the seven essential grains. Great vats of oil were wheeled out in anticipation of the night-long celebrations. The royal kitchens were in clouds of steam, hissing and sputtering with vegetarian and non-vegetarian fare.

Jewellers decided they would unlock vaults and bring out their finest designs to bedazzle the new brides Sita and Urmilla and mark the arrival of their beloved princes Rama and Lakshmana.

The weavers stopped short on their looms and decided to give away yards of stocked cloth that was meant for the next season. Women wove jasmines into flower garlands for the hair at the speed of lightning with their nimble fingers, while the bangle sellers brought out the auspicious green gemmed bangles for every virgin in the street whose mother wanted her to find a suitable boy. The sweet vendors were pleading with basket weavers to hurry up with the containers of their many-coloured sweets that were being handed to everyone at the joyous news.

Kaikeyi, the king's favourite queen, was hastening her maids-in-waiting to select a rainbow of accessories; Sumitra was thrilled to hear her son Lakshmana was returning home, and that he was bringing her a daughter-in-law! Shatrughuna, Lakshmana's twin, was eagerly awaiting his brothers' return and wanted to fill a vast chronicle with information on how Rama and Lakshmana vanquished the demons.

Kausalya, Rama's birth mother, was offering prayers and thanks to her gods in her personal shrine room with ardent devotion when Dasaratha came in. It was customary that at the three points of the sun in a day—sunrise, noon and sunset—the husband would appear, and the eldest wife would perform *aarati* and salute him, honouring him for granting her longevity through his own long life. Dasaratha was beaming with a quiet joy as the flame of the camphor from the aarati was waved three times, clockwise around his face. She bent down and touched his feet and he took the vermilion dust from the aarati tray and placed a dot on her forehead. In his other hand, he had a silk parchment scroll bearing his royal seal. Kaikeyi and Sumitra, the younger wives also bowed, touched his feet and he placed a dot on their foreheads as well. Bharatha and Shatrughuna followed. Then Dasaratha looked at his sons and said, 'Bharatha, after Rama, you are the eldest in the kingdom. My only living father-in-law, your grandfather, the king of Keykeya must be given these joyous tidings. You are the one who is most suited to perform this grand duty. Your chariot is waiting and is laden with gifts for my beloved family of Keykeya. I would have gone myself, but we must get things ready for Sage Viswamithra and our beloved Rama and Lakshmana. If you hurry, you could return early to be part of all the ceremonies.' Then, holding out the scroll, he said: 'Bharatha, take all your mothers' and their favourite gods' blessings. Be the bearer of this scroll and hand it to your grandfather when he is in the presence of the priests. Never lose sight of it on your journey. Return with his royal seal of receipt.'

Hearing his father's words, Bharatha suddenly felt that from a boy, he had become a man with the honour of a responsibility, his father, the king, had given him. Kaikeyi was the first to urge him to hurry in fulfilling his father's command. But, more importantly, she said: 'Beloved and only son, you must return soon. Otherwise, you will be sorely disappointed not to be in our Rama's company long enough.'

Bharatha took his leave and left. That afternoon, there was no siesta after lunch in Ayodhya. Everyone was preparing for the celebrations. Particularly the musicians composing new ragas and talas.

The elephants were bathed and bedecked for Rama's return. Their ornaments were blazing like torches as the sun began its journey towards rest.

Just as the sun had turned into a crimson ball sinking into the west, great curved trumpets blew from Ayodhya's watchtowers. They could see the procession, Rama and Lakshmana leading it with their brides, and Sage Viswamithra by their side. And then the escorts and revellers from Mithila. Now that Mithila had had its moment in ecstatic celebration, Ayodhya did not want to be left behind. Although Rama had vanquished the rakshasa Tataka and her son, won the tournament and wed Sita, he did not return to his father's kingdom as a victor. He considered the real glory was in the teachings of Viswamithra. In the face of triumph, there must be humility. From Sita, he learned that in the wake of great joy, one must experience the sorrow of fleeting time, and so think positive thoughts.

Ayodhya's people watched Rama's gentle smile. They knew their prince had journeyed far, and his bride must see his people as hospitable. So they decided to contain their excitement to ensure that their princes and their brides and the great Viswamithra were assured of some quiet before a whole new era unravelled the next day.

Dasaratha slept in Kaikeyi's palace that night. She knew how excitedly he had waited for Rama's safe return, and the sheer relief from that had brought on a slight headache. Kaikeyi soothed Dasaratha with songs that she had composed for Rama as a child. In fact, she loved Rama like her very own. Both Dasaratha and she remembered the silly rhymes they would sing to encourage the princes' first words, the games that they created for the boys to test their learning in different subjects. Kaikeyi was loving and loveable and had kept Dasaratha enchanted for all the years they had been married. Like the other queens, she had given him a son, Bharatha, but unlike the others, she alone had the key to his heart.

Dasaratha indulged in the affections of his favourite wife and queen and, on Rama's homecoming, felt a great peace in his heart.

He awoke early in the morning to the chanting of the Brahmins.

As he stirred from his bed, he gazed at Kaikeyi, sleeping. 'How tender her heart is through all these years. How she rejoices Rama's homecoming as if he were her own flesh and blood! I am truly blessed to have such peace-loving wives,' he murmured as he bent his head to gently kiss her ear.

He caught his reflection in the shining brass banner that functioned as a mirror. His chin sagged and his cheeks were jowls. Dasaratha, great as he was, could not help being vain. 'What!' he exclaimed in his thoughts. 'Where has time taken away the youth from my face?!' He rose from the bed and saw his body. He felt the burden of age. He sighed. But today was a new day, and he had arranged to meet Rama in his royal chamber.

As he was being dressed to receive his son, Dasaratha thought of something. A new light sprang into his eyes. Rama came at the appointed moment and touched his father's feet to accept his blessings.

'Now we will speak as father and son, man to man,' Dasaratha said beaming. Rama told him of how his world view had changed following the encounter with the rakshasas, meeting the people in the jungle as well as the people of Mithila. Dasaratha kept asking Rama questions about various things that ranged from the layout of the forest to the most valued thing in Mithila. An hour went by in this manner. Dasaratha was satisfied. He called in his chief minister and looking directly into Rama's eyes said: 'Rama, my beloved son, you will be crowned king tomorrow, on the full moon'. 'But father, you are and will always be the beloved king of the people of Ayodhya. I will only be your able assistant,' Rama replied, genuinely surprised at his father's command. Dasaratha's beaming and almost defiant response was: 'I have decided, Rama, the time has come.' With that, to seal his words of intention and action, he took the shawl from across his shoulders and placed it like a garland around Rama's neck. Dasaratha felt a great load lighten, for at last he had found the perfect heir, to what was in his lifetime, the perfect kingdom.

By midmorning, the news was official that Rama was to be crowned king within the next twenty-four hours. This was the biggest celebration that Ayodhya could have over Mithila! The priests were going about setting horoscopes for the kingship, the generals were planning processions and military drills for the coronation ceremony, and there was drumming and dancing throughout the day in the streets.

Kaikeyi was in her palace, getting her singing attendants to rehearse a new song she had composed for Rama's coronation. As they excelled with each rehearsal, she would take off a precious jewel from her neck, arm or waist and present it to them with an exclamation of pure joy.

She didn't notice how her shoulder was being shaken by Kooni, the hunchback maid from Keykeya, whom she had brought with her when she married Dasaratha. Kaikeyi was too absorbed in directing the performers, but suddenly Kooni screamed, bringing the rehearsal and air of merriment to a halt. 'What is the matter with you all?!

Your death knell is pronounced, and you all are behaving as if you have all the time on earth!'

Kaikeyi still intent on completing the rehearsal said 'Lovely Kooni, come let me stroke your back. I must finish this rehearsal.'

You beautiful, most innocent and loveliest of duped queens, I am here to shake you up from your stupor. Rama is being crowned king, Sita is his wife, and you will be treated like a slave in all the palaces because you are so gullible,' rebuked Kooni.

'You silly old thing, what are you on about! Of course we are preparing for Rama's coronation with this special song I have composed! Summoning her singers and dancers Kaikeyi said: 'Now come on girls, let's sing it once again nicely for Kooni so she doesn't feel left out. Maybe we will even have a part in it for her!'

Who knows what Kooni felt. In a fit of venomous rage, Kooni flung down the gold water jar, the singing attendants screamed and ran out in a fluster, leaving Kooni and Kaikeyi alone.

Kaikeyi knew that Kooni missed home, and sometimes these outbursts were an indication of how she had not had time alone with her beloved queen. So Kaikeyi decided to indulge her.

'Don't think you can read my mind,' Kooni scowled, 'I'm not a child, I will not be pacified.'

'Well, if you are not a child then you must conduct yourself according to the wisdom of your age and your position,' said Kaikeyi with some authority.

'Position! My position! My only position is to protect you and now you are so smeared by the sleaze of the man you married that you cannot even see what is wrong from right!' bayed Kooni again.

'Enough! I've had enough of your games about loyalty! My loyalty is to my husband and his kingdom. Kooni, what a joyous occasion this is that our son . . .'

'Not *your* son . . .'

'Rama is going to be crowned king! What a blessed time we live in!'

'Listen to me Kaikeyi. I know the secrets of your birth, your family, your marriage. I know the story of your life. I also know what you hold as the greatest jewel in your marriage to your husband . . .'

'What do you mean?' Kaikeyi asked, faltering.

Kooni swooped into that moment of faltering, and like a kite's talons, ripped into the body of secrets that Kaikeyi held most dear.

'This is why I say, my beloved queen, beware. If I am about to say anything that is harmful, then strike me dead. Come, your head is hot; let me soothe it with your favourite potion.' Saying that, Kooni took out an ampule containing a fragrance reminiscent of Keykeya and began smoothing it across Kaikeyi's temples and the nape of her neck. As Kaikeyi breathed in the vapours of her youth and childhood, Kooni began:

'Do you remember that fatal battle when your father sent you as Dasaratha's charioteer? How bravely you heaved the chariot wheel out of the rut in the mud track while he was fighting his foes. You were so strong and fierce then Kaikeyi, it must come back. Remember when your father gave your hand in marriage . . .'

'Yes,' said Kaikeyi, her eyes drooping, 'I remember telling Dasaratha I would marry only if he always told me the truth and that I would hold no secret from him.'

'So, why then in front of all of us did he tell *your* son Bharatha to go bade greetings to your father, when Rama was about to arrive?'

'Because he needed to send word to my father . . .' Kaikeyi's eyelids were drooping and she was muttering.

'Or was it something else? Did you see the scroll he sent?' asked Kooni as she found the nerve along Kaikeyi's neck that often gave her pain and cricked it.

'No . . .' said Kaikeyi, weak with relief.

'In that scroll should have been your father's word of honour signed with Dasaratha's that when Bharatha comes of age, he will be the king . . .'

'But Rama . . .' said Kaikeyi, with fragrant vapours of confusion clouding her brain.

'Never mind that, I was in the secret chamber when Dasaratha and your father made this contract. Nobody else is aware of it. Not even you. Kaikeyi, destiny is in your hands. Think of the truth.'

'Dasaratha and I married the truth,' Kaikeyi said somnambulistically.

'Then think again, beautiful one, your loyalty has been betrayed.'

8

An Ocean of Churning Events

It can never be known what compels us to do certain things. So it must be said of Kooni. She had nothing to gain personally from diverting Kaikeyi's celebration of Rama's coronation. Kooni was old now, and perhaps she felt homesick, but seeing Kaikeyi so well settled in Ayodhya, she probably felt she would never be released from her service. Perhaps Kooni felt if she could not have peace and happiness, then why should everyone else? Maybe she was just in a bad mood when she entered Kaikeyi's palace, and seeing the queen looking so beautifully happy in the company of her attendants made her lonely, and once she lashed out in a bad mood it created a vortex she could not get out of, and as she spiralled downward into hatred, she took the queen with her. We all get into these negative moods, and the important thing is to reason ourselves out of a bad mood or, even better, to have someone who can snap us out of our self-indulgence. All the situation really needed was for one of the attendants to say: 'Kooni! Get a life!' or indeed for Kaikeyi to say it. But no one had the guts. So whatever Kooni's intention was, she went at it with such force that it changed the whole course of events.

By the afternoon, in spite of the merriment in the streets, the officials were in meeting after meeting, setting out a tight timetable of events for the next day's coronation that culminated in the rising of the full moon. Dasaratha was at each of these meetings, listening to summaries that he would question, add to, and ultimately approve. Rama and Sita were instructed to fast, rest early in separate apartments and be anointed at 4 a.m., for all the ceremonies that would follow.

By early evening, Dasaratha wished to have one last council with Rama. Rama was amazed at the speed with which his father had worked and expressed his deep gratitude. Dasaratha raised his bowed head and gazing into his son's calm eyes said: 'This must be done. I sometimes dream strange things that influence the way I think in the day. Your mind is not muddled by these things; it is pure, and you can see clearly. You are the best to lead the way. Rama, remember to keep the ones who are dear to you close, but keep those who remain at a distance even closer, as they may mean you harm.' Rama was perplexed to see his father succumb to such suspicions. Was this a sign of age, and therefore vulnerability? Then, in a flash, Dasaratha was himself again. 'So, my beloved Rama, what joy you have brought to this kingdom with your wife Sita, and now nothing can stop the Ishvaku clan from rising with solar strength!'

Dasaratha had a few more duties to complete before retiring to his palace. At every task he completed, he could not help but feel the relief, that this was the last time he would be the sole authority. From now on, it would be Rama. He had ruled for some forty years, and a wave of nostalgia slowly crept over him as he remembered each of his campaigns and his weddings to his beautiful and faithful wives. By the time he looked up from his parchments, the sun had long sunk into the west and night had fallen.

As he rose to go to his apartments, a delicate piece of silk encrusted with gems fell from one of the scrolls he was reading. It was a love poem that Kaikeyi had embroidered on the silk fragment all those years ago:

> Through all the seasons that this earth will know,
> you are the morning glory of my heart.
> Rescue me from this listless yearning,
> o tender creeper of love, never keep us apart.

Dasaratha sighed. A tear crept down his face. Yes, the exquisite Kaikeyi had truly stolen his heart.

So instead of walking to his palace, he decided to stroll across to Kaikeyi's. A senior messenger brought the news that Bharatha had safely reached his grandfather's kingdom of Keykeya. Dasaratha was relieved. Now he could go and rejoice with Kaikeyi, not too late though, because tomorrow was the big day.

When he went to her palace, it was unlit. 'Of course! She must have given everyone an early night, so they wake up fresh tomorrow,' Dasaratha thought. He was growing feverish with excitement that after this night, he would be a free man.

He went to her inner bed chamber. All was dark, and he was about to turn and leave when he stepped on something. He bent to pick it up, and as his eyes grew accustomed to the dark, he discovered it was the necklace that he had given Kaikeyi at the birth of the princes. 'What could have brought this about?' he wondered. Half playful, he started calling out, 'Kaikeyi? Kaikeyi! Where are you? This isn't some kind of game you are playing with me, are you? Okay . . . Okay then, just give me some clues.' He continued in this vein until Kaikeyi stirred and sat up. Dasaratha quickly lit a lamp and held it out, saying, 'My Darling! My beautiful one! You're not well. I told you to contain this excitement of yours. Now look! You've exhausted yourself. How will that make Rama feel?' he cajoled her.

'Don't you dare talk to me!' Kaikeyi thundered. Her hair stood out in smoky coils, and as Dasaratha trembled and brought the lamp closer to her, he could see her eyes were sunken and sore from constant weeping. He stretched out his hand that held the necklace and tried to touch her cheek; she caught the clasp of the necklace and, pulling it out of his hand, struck it against the wall, rubies flying like drops of blood.

'You stole my youth with your sweet promises, and now, as I'm ageing, I have to face this horror of deceit! O Dasaratha how could you!'

Dasaratha's knees were growing weak. He placed the lamp on a table and tried to steady himself. He tried to find his voice to say something that might chase this apparition away. But dry dust was all he felt in his throat.

'Do you remember that battle when I saved you, as your charioteer . . .' she began.

'Of course, Kaikeyi, but why is all that coming up now?' pleaded Dasaratha, as he began to see the phantoms of his nightmares right before his eyes. The only truth was that Rama was the best king for Ayodhya; surely she knew that? Dasaratha blinked. Words stuck like pins in his throat. Had she not always understood him? He blinked again.

'Why are you so afraid? Because you have hidden the truth? Dasaratha, our love and marriage was based on the promise that you would never deceive me. Now, you have broken my heart. But I'll strike back. Do you remember those two boons you offered me when I saved your life? Well, if you are truly the King of Kings then you must honour them now.'

'Ask for anything Kai. You know I will grant you anything, my most beloved . . .'

'Enough of all that nonsense! The first boon: Rama must be exiled from this kingdom for thirteen years; the second boon: Bharatha must be crowned the king. Let me see how you honour your words.' She sealed his fate.

Anybody who was there might have wondered if it was a peacock wailing or a cat in pain, had they heard the cry from Dasaratha's throat. He fell to the ground. And as he was falling, he couldn't help asking himself, was this a dream? He had been so jubilant a few moments ago, so nimble of step waiting for tomorrow. But now, a vice-like grip had seized his limbs, and although words ran like a script in his head, he could only release the sounds of a baying animal. He was struck dumb. Hours passed as he lay like this.

Dasaratha's trusted chief minister, realizing something must be wrong when the king did not appear for the morning chants to awaken the gods especially on the day of the coronation, went to seek him, and found him in a pitiable condition.

All the king could say was 'Rrrr . . .' The chief minister could not imagine what had happened. But Kaikeyi, dressed in all the finery befitting a queen for the coronation said: 'The king is indisposed, can't you see? He has asked me to interpret for him.'

Dasaratha became even more agitated and now began to twitch violently. The pain in his heart was growing even more severe, and his mouth foamed. Kaikeyi continued, 'As all the plans for the coronation are set, everything should proceed accordingly. Only, you will have a different king. It will be MY son Bharatha. This is the word of honour that the King of Kings has given.'

The chief minister felt the vein in the right side of his head pounding like a hammer on a block. What was he to do? Place the king in a comfortable position, or plead with his favourite Queen to reconsider what she had just said? And then there were Rama and Sita, waiting, along with all the people and arrangements that had been set like clockwork for the whole day.

He tried lifting the old king, but found his body was unbearably rigid. The minister realized that the only solace for his agony would be the sight of Rama.

Rama was waiting for his father's blessings, and, not knowing what to expect, rushed to Kaikeyi's palace. He had never seen anyone in this condition. Here was his father, the King of Kings, a crumpled heap on the floor, twitching and gibbering incoherently. Rama held his father's head. He could feel the tears running like a river; the tears of an old man stung with pain and the most unexpected betrayal. Kaikeyi still commanded the scene as if she had an entire audience before her: 'Rama, how churlish of you not to take my blessings. I'll forgive you this time. But as your father is incoherent, I must give you his orders. You are from this instance exiled from the kingdom for thirteen years. *My* son Bharatha will be crowned king.'

Rama could not grasp the scale of this command, but he knew that if that was what his father's favourite wife and queen commanded, then it was as good as having come from his father. Distressed by Dasaratha's condition, he could not interpret the situation in any other way. Although he was confused by the sudden change in events, it paled in comparison to his concern for his father's condition.

Rama went to Kaikeyi to take her blessings, but she turned her back on him. The minister beckoned him to leave and inform his mother, Kausalya, the senior queen. Rama also went to Sita to tell her the news. Everyone in the family gathered in Kaikeyi's palace and placed the king in a more comfortable position. Kaikeyi was insistent that he was removed from her palace so that it could be decorated and be free of any signs of grief. As Kaikeyi was loved by most in the past, and although her manner seemed strange, people, numbed by grief at the king's condition, obeyed her commands. The royal physicians administered herbs that soothed the king's rigid muscles and sent him to sleep, finally putting a stop to his weeping.

Everyone in Ayodhya was in turmoil. They were anticipating the greatest event of their lifetime, not an ocean of churning events. No one could understand what to do next. Kooni sounded like a hyena as she laughed and prepared her betel nut and leaves, announcing: 'See, Bharatha of Keykeya will be king!' People who heard her thought she too was so enveloped in grief that she was being ironic. Meanwhile, Kaikeyi kept imagining she had great audiences coming to bestow accolades on her as the queen mother and had to be reminded by her faithful attendants that Bharatha had no news of what had happened and was not yet crowned king. This subdued her somewhat.

Rama was the only one who knew what he had to do next. He had been ordered to leave the kingdom. So, after consoling his mother Kausalya and leaving her in Sita's care, he went to his apartment and removed every symbol on his body that indicated his royalty. Then tying his hair like a forest dweller, he unpacked his dhoti of bark and wore it. With a bare torso and bare feet, he took one last look at the apartment that he had known since his childhood. 'Strange,' he thought, 'to leave everything so familiar, so certain, so suddenly. I will make the Unknown my friend.' So resolved, he went to bid farewell to his mother. Kausalya, seeing him in a forest dweller's attire, fainted. Sita, who was still dressed in her royal garments, revived the queen. Rama was relieved he could leave his dear, kind mother in the capable care of Sita. He paused for a moment and gazed at Sita and said, 'We have lived a lifetime from the days of our wedding to this moment. True, it has been cut short. But having you so close in my heart will remind me to return. Look after my dear mother who has borne much in these past few hours. Queen Kaikeyi has ordered that I be exiled from this kingdom for thirteen years . . .' He had said as much as his breeding had allowed him to deliver with calm. But, looking into Sita's eyes, he could not hold back his tears.

Sita was furious. 'Rama,' her eyes sparked fire into her words, 'did you think I would stay behind and leave you to venture ahead alone? Yes, I respect your mother deeply, but my vows of companionship were for us to share each other's hardships and celebrations. That is how we care for our parents.'

'But Sita,' Rama protested, 'the forests and the dangers that lurk there . . . I will never forgive myself should anything happen to you.'

'Rama! There are so many ifs and buts. We are not sure from one moment to the next what can happen in our lives. At least if we are together, we will have spent time with each other, and who knows how things will unravel? Now come, put away these thoughts. I love you Rama, and with you I will go.'

Rama steeled himself one last time and said, 'But this order is only for me. I would not like to disobey my father in any respect, more so since he is so grieved.'

Sita tore the ancestral necklace off its clasp and placed it at Kausalya's feet. She took her mother-in-law's blessings and said: 'Rama, I was not brought up to quarrel, so I will not. But you cannot stop me from accompanying you into exile, as I am determined to. Also, there are many histories and stories about people like us, and I am certain that in every retelling of the Ramayana, Sita decides to go to the forest. Otherwise, how will the future generations know what happened, and if there is a story to tell!'

Rama was stumped. Sita had scored the ultimate point. Who knows, Valmiki, who had developed the power of foresight, and in his meditations could see how the whole story was to take place. As the epic poet, he realized Sita with her love for Rama, would choose to be with him in exile.

It wasn't long before Lakshmana appeared, dressed just like Rama, took his mother's blessings, and said: 'Brother, surely you would not expect me to stay here in this basket of snakes? No pastime in the palace would suit me, save being beside you and Sita. If you do not let me come, I will drown myself in the Sarayu, I swear.' Poor Rama. What a predicament! To be loved and yet cast out from making any decision, because he was overruled. All he knew was that time was running out. So he took one last look at all the beloved faces around him and strode out of the archways. Sita and Lakshmana followed him to the palace gates. It was thronging with the people of Ayodhya, all in tears, all deciding to join him in exile, so that Kaikeyi could have an empty kingdom to rule.

What a sight it was.

Kanda IV

9

Crossing a River, Entering Exile

That night, all the people of Ayodhya slept at the banks of the Sarayu; tired not from following Rama and Sita into exile, but from the grief that now descended into their hearts. The wise minister, summoned by Rama, got a boat and while everyone was asleep, rowed them away to the far bank that skirted the forests. The three of them walked silently as day broke and the birds began their dawn chorus. When they came to a clearing, they discovered a hill, a good vantage point, and Lakshmana, Rama and Sita climbed it to have a rest. They must have barely shut their eyes when the sun's rays stretched wide across the sky. A new energy brought on by an uncertain new life crept into them. They could not sleep.

Lakshmana was watching the clearing down below like a hawk. Suddenly in the distance, he saw a crowd and signalled to Rama. It could not be the people of Ayodhya.

They would not have found enough boats overnight. And as this crowd approached, it seemed from where Rama and Lakshmana's perch was, to be an assembly of ascetic men with their brother Bharatha leading them. Lakshmana, spurred to protect Rama and Sita, and grieving at the way they were cast out by Kaikeyi, hissed between clenched teeth: 'Look brother! How he has armed himself with ascetics so that I cannot attack him. He has come to laugh at you and push you further away from sight and sense. Let him come near!' Rama sighed gently and said: 'Lakshmana, I know how hurt you are on my behalf. But let that not come in the way of calm judgment. Especially of any person, whether it is our brother or any other. In your anger, you have already killed him from this distance. Beware of it. This is the time our true nature is on test. Let him approach, let us greet him, let him speak, then make up your mind about his intention. Why lose a friend and gain a foe?'

Lakshmana wiped away a tear and thought: 'How magnanimous Rama truly is! What a great injustice is done to him by sending him out on this exile for thirteen years!' Rama had turned his head away, but Sita spoke to Lakshmana: 'Rama, our beloved brother, hurts on your behalf with anger and pain. Know this Lakshmana; you are his dearest companion, transcending this world of petty blows. Let us each remember that love fortifies everything; and should an enemy seize us now, even kill us, the truth of our purpose to love will bring a change in this world.'

By now Bharatha had seen Rama and Lakshmana and approached them. He was wearing tree bark, the sign of an ascetic, not a warrior prince and fell at the feet of Rama. When Rama raised him from the ground, he saw before him a man whose soul was in torment. Bharatha blurted out that he had disowned his mother Kaikeyi, had never known of her vicious plans of exiling Rama, and had come to request Rama to ascend the throne. Rama consoled his brother's outpouring and knew how sincere he was. But he said he must honour his father's words. 'But it was my mother who spoke them! They are worthless!'

Rama only said: 'Her words as the king's wife are as good as my own mother's, and our father's.'

The pleading from Bharatha, for Rama to return, went on for most of the day. When the sun began to set, Rama said calmly, 'Dear Bharatha, I have always looked upon you as a part of myself. You are now king of Ayodhya by the wisdom of our father's past actions. That is the truth. You must rule by example.' Bharatha interjected: 'It's not the truth. It's my mother's untimely conniving to suit her own needs,' and he wept bitterly at how severed he felt from every memory of childhood and his friendship with Rama.

But, Bharatha recognized the truth of what Rama said and the consequences now being faced by these brothers in matters of kingship. 'But I will only return if you offer me your sandals. I will place them on the throne and be an agency of government. I will wait for your return. If you do not return on the day these thirteen years end, I will light a fire and enter it. I would have done my duty to you, my father, and in your words, to our people. You are the rightful king of Ayodhya.'

Rama offered his wooden sandals and as the sun turned a light orange, the colour of the fire of renunciation where all past desires burn away, Bharatha set out to return to Ayodhya, carrying the sandals on his head.

Sita watched him go and wondered: 'Will his mother not tempt him again? He has not once thought of himself, but only of Rama. How different his ambitions are from Queen Kaikeyi's! The kingdom and its people, disappear into nothingness when he asks to serve only the beloved Rama! How could he have drunk his mother's milk! Why did the king send him away at the time of the coronation? Seems strange. Much as these brothers are endowed with respect for their father and mothers, there is a profound wisdom in their core. It is strong enough for them to know the difference between what is just and unjust. Hail Ayodhya! You opened your doors to me as a daughter of this kingdom when I married Rama. More than anything, I will be true to my love for him. Wish you well, good brother Bharatha.'

It turned to night. It was a full moon night. It would have been the night of the coronation. In that luminous dark, all Bharatha was thinking of was his parting from Rama and the lost days of their childhood together. Had Rama really forgiven him, he wondered. Just at that moment, he tripped on a sharp stone and cried out 'Rama!' as one of the sandals flew out of his hands.

'Oh! Rama! What have I done? I was so full of my own sentimental thoughts that now I cannot even carry out the task I set myself. What is the point of living if I cannot find your sandal? O heat of the earth, burn me up now!' As he was thinking these anguished thoughts, a messenger came riding fast and sped him away to the king's bedside.

By the time Bharatha arrived by his father's side, the King of Kings was a slip of a man wasted away by the events not of years, but the last twelve hours. By the time he touched his father's feet, the king groaned and was dead. Bharatha was totally bereft. He had never thought that when his father gave him the responsibility of being a royal messenger to the king of Keykeya, it would entail lighting the funeral pyre. He kept remembering Rama's serenity, and it contained him from jumping into the funeral pyre and ending it all, as he was tempted to, because he had nothing to do with the turn of events. He kept reasoning with himself that this was the symptom of grief. But he could not, no matter how he was counselled; he could not bear to stand in the same space as Kaikeyi. He had always been brought up to revere his parents. But his greater wisdom and intuition made him distinguish between a parent who adhered to the truth, and a parent who gave way to greed fed by false testimonies, being so oblivious to the grief of others in gaining satisfaction for herself.

Valmiki, as the seer of events in the future, and the author of the work, was quite insistent on this from his own experience when he led his life as Ratnakar. He realized that had it not been for Narada, who made him see the truth as it was, blindly following someone, including one's own family, can only lead to harm. Hold fast to the truth, and the good parent will guide you.

Bharatha knew that Rama was still across the riverbank and could not resist delivering the news of their beloved father's death. So he went with a new resolve, possibly secretly hoping Rama might return. But people had noticed a change in Bharatha. He looked much older than his years. He wore the garb of a monk. At first, they thought this was a necessary passing phase for someone so young who is grieving. Bharatha took the urn of his father's ashes and went in search of Rama again. This time Lakshmana greeted him without any doubt. But when the three brothers gazed at the remains of their father held in an urn full of ashes, all their memories of childhood leapt up like the blazing flames of a funeral pyre. There were many happy memories, and the sheer agony of recalling them for Bharatha was that Kaikeyi was so much a vivid part of them for all the brothers. Visions of his mother would flare up, and he would clench his fists in rage. Rama knew what Bharatha was going through. For Rama, the pain was not so sharp. He held his brother close to say: 'Let us remember that we were brought up together in the same family, and our love is our eternal bond. No one can come between us.' That was reassurance enough. Both brothers looked at each other for what would be the last time in their youth. The bend in the river created fierce currents. Rama, Sita and Lakshmana had crossed the river into a period of exile by the order of Kaikeyi. Bharatha too entered an inner exile of rejecting anything sentimental. He took to governing the kingdom, only in the service of Rama.

News spread like wildfire, and people wondered whether this would make Ayodhya vulnerable to attack. But the power of its commercial trade was deemed strong and worthwhile, and the fact that an ascetic ruler governed it in the people's interests only gained greater praise. To fight against such a ruler would be a crass destruction of ethical values.

The more interesting news that reached Lanka of course was that Rama had been exiled to live in the forest. Ravana cackled and chuckled with triumphant laughter. Lightning bristled in the sky, not from Indra's thunderbolt, but the grinding of Ravana's teeth.

But Ravana wanted to be sure if this news was true. He could not disclose his real intention. Was Sita left alone in the Ayodhya palace? He schemed night and day on how to conceal his real desire of wanting to find out about Sita. Finally, he deftly sent his spies on a mission to find out if the news about Rama in exile was fact. He sent them via different routes to Ayodhya, some with sheer magic that made them invisible, some in disguise, but none as an envoy bearing condolences.

The strange and interesting fact about rakshasas, or dark forces, is that while they stir a lot of ill feelings, and terrorize people, they can't bear being in places where there is suffering, particularly when the human spirit tries to endure and overcome difficult circumstances. So when Ravana's rakshasa spies came as ghouls and magic spirits wanting to wreak a little havoc in Ayodhya for fun, they were stunned to find Ayodhya mourning. People went about their business after the king's death with dignity and respected all the rites of the day as when he was living, according to Bharatha's governance. Ravana's spies found this distasteful, as no one seemed vulnerable to attack. There was some strong soul force that stirred in the heart of Ayodhya. On enquiring by means of various disguises across Ayodhya, the spies discovered that Sita too had left.

They flew back to Ravana, glad to be rid of a place where the human spirit showed so much courage. The spies couldn't bear it. But of course, there was a whole new set of orders issued when Ravana heard the news. He was furious! How dare Sita display this kind of love for a useless human who could not even crown himself king? What was the use of being young and handsome? How foolish of him to take her through the dangers of exile, Ravana raved in his head. The order he barked out was: 'Go this instant and start looking for them in the forests! Don't you dare touch either of them. I will deal with the situation once you return with your reports.' Ravana suspected that while these spies were good, they weren't suitable for the job that he really had in mind. Besides, they continually returned to him with the news: 'Your Imperial Grace! Rama that coward is in a part of the forest that is impenetrable.'

'Now what good was the fine art of black magic if you hollow skulls can't find out where they are!' exploded Ravana. He knew one of his clans that would know the workings of his mind without an exchange of words. Secrecy was ultimate in the game that Ravana had in mind. He merely sent a thought wave to his sister Soorpanakha.

She was a deadly rakshasa, fiercely intelligent, and could get bored very easily. Unfortunately for us, in her leisure time she liked devising ways of killing different kinds of creatures. She lived in the depths of the forests and had never been challenged and was left free to do as she pleased. As a result, she wasn't much fun to be with, even amongst the rakshasa clan. They did not enjoy her visiting them on holidays when she ran out of creatures to kill. They humoured her naturally, because she was Ravana's sister, and being subject to her wishes could win them the favour of their mighty emperor.

Deep in the wilderness, she could sense that Ravana was sending her a thought wave. She decided she would take her time answering it as Ravana had completely neglected her over the last few years.

10

So Many Kinds of Love

It took Rama, Sita and Lakshmana a matter of months to master the art of living in exile. Naturally, their life was simple. As they travelled through the forests, they encountered different kinds of birdsong; Sita would note the changing flora and fauna, marking the beginning and turn of a season, and time. They met travellers, and never once disclosed their identity so that they could meet life as it is, not as if it was a royal pageant. They decided that they would camp in a particular forest for at least six months and then move on.

A few years passed, and Rama was grateful to have Sita beside him. She made him see things in a different light. Lakshmana offered other perspectives on viewing life. It made him realize all the more the different kinds of habitats, not only of animals but of tribes, people who lived rejecting society or conventions of a community, and how people might be compelled to act in certain ways according to their circumstances. They met boatmen, fishermen, hunters and ascetics, but one encounter was truly different.

After Bharatha's departure, Rama, Sita and Lakshmana could not bear being in the forest known as Chitrakuta. It seemed the closure of one chapter and they decided to move to another forest. The season was also turning. It was no longer fresh, holding the breath of *basant*'s spring and new blossom. With the rising heat and humidity, flowers hung heavy, their scent strong and heady, but drooped lifelessly in a short while. On other trees, it was time when fruit were ripening. The buffaloes drove themselves into ponds and lakes to keep cool, slick with mud. It was a job for forest dwellers and villagers alike to get the buffaloes out of their water stations so that they could be milked! This was the season of Greeshma. Afternoons were hot and sultry when the best thing to do was slip into a heavy sleep and sweat. On waking, the southern breeze would dry the beads of sweat and that kept one cool.

The three of them now entered a forest. It seemed clearer than the ones they had just travelled. There were groves of clusters of five different kinds of trees. Vata (*ficus benghalensis, Banyan*), Ashvattha (*ficus religiosa, Peepal*), Bilva (*aegle marmelos, Bengal Quince*), Amalaki (*phyllanthus emblica, Indian Gooseberry, Amla*), Ashoka (*Saraca asoca, Ashok*), Udumbara (*ficus racemosa, Cluster Fig, Gular*), Nimba (*Azadirachta indica, Neem*) and gave the forest its name: Panchavati. Many were with low boughs and branches that spread wide and close on the ground.

Lakshmana swiftly used the low boughs as a scaffold and with Rama, they built two dwellings; Lakshmana's camouflaged watchtower was attached to his dwelling. Panchavati was so calm after all they had been through, and Sita cheerfully made this her home. She began to name plants and flowers and their fruits. Rama would take in the late afternoon flurry of birdsong and squirrel fights and tap a soft percussive rhythm on his bow to the low grizzle of tigers in the distance.

One day, he was completely captivated by the emerald, green dance of the parrots. Their shrieks were echoing in response to the mating calls of the monkeys. In the dappled sunlight, the green wings and bright pink beaks of the parrots darting through the trees was an enchanting choreography. Absorbed in this scene, he must have let his guard slip.

Someone, unknown to any of them, was watching him.

It so happened that there was a visitor in Panchavati. She was a demon who wanted to investigate the calm of the forest and demolish it. That was her nature and her job description as a professional demon rakshasa. But she caught sight of Rama. 'Now *he* is worth my attention,' she thought. It was Soorpanakha. She did not want to eat him, even though eating while demolishing was part of the perks of her job; instead, she wanted to approach Rama as a lover. What amazing courage. She was going against her nature and her job description. In the midst of the calm that Rama, Sita and Lakshmana had created, she experienced human feelings of joy stir within her. Feeling happiness she had not known before, she wanted to share it, in her way, by making an offer of love of a different kind.

Love is blind, we have heard before; often we are blinded by our own love, thinking that the object of our love must love us back. The slight problem is that demons and humans have different attractions. Humans are fussy about good looks. Humans don't like a 'come as you are person' offering love. They like it all dressed up. Soorpanakha knew this about humans. She looked at herself, what did she look like?

She had a face that was shaped like a circle about sixteen feet in diameter. Her mouth was another circle about three feet in diameter when shut. When it opened, there was one sabretooth that could stretch like a telescope to a length of twenty feet. She had one eye in the centre of her forehead. Below the eye was a bulbous nose. Her lips were a lush red, darkened by the blood of the freshly killed animals and humans that she had flung into her mouth on one of her demolition patrols. She had no neck and her head was on top of a mountain of a body that could be drawn in six circles, each wider than the other. Strangely, although her feet looked large and heavy with curving toenails that were useful in gouging the intestines from her prey, she was light-footed. Her toes faced backwards, and her heels faced forwards. She had to be light on her feet to capture her prey. This wasn't all. Her hair was twenty-nine and three-quarter feet long. In its knots and tangles were mud and slime, and snails and scorpions, and water snakes. From her ears, the wax stood out like fossilized cones, hosting creatures that are now well extinct.

Yes, it does take courage to go up to someone and insist on having their love, when all that person would feel is the shock of death!

But Soorpanakha was a senior mistress rakshasa demon in the art of illusion and disguise. After all, she was the sister of her favourite and imperial brother Ravana.

Rama, transfixed by the dance of the parrots suddenly caught Sita mischievously looking at him as if to say, 'That was the way you looked at me when our eyes met on that street in Mithila! Now, something else has caught your attention I can see!' He acknowledged her thought by grinning and as he pointed to the parrots, suddenly his senses were filled with an opiate perfume. And then, she appeared. Soorpanakha. But not the way you and I saw her a few moments ago. She was now the queen of distraction. She was 5 feet tall and had doe-like eyes heavily lined with kohl so the whites of her eyes looked like crescent moons. Her lips were red with the dye of betel nut leaves. Her hair was lustrous in ebony tresses and reached down to her full hips, swinging like a pendulum when she walked. She was dressed in the finest yellow silk from her waist to her feet. Her bodice was a parrot green silk embroidered with precious diamonds and rubies encircled in paisleys of pearls. Around her shoulders, she had a diaphanous silk dupatta in a mother-of-pearl colour that made her shoulders gleam with the colours of the rainbow in the afternoon light.

She wore long earrings that hung lightly from her ears to her long, marble-smooth neck. To match, her necklaces were in gold and rubies, and although one could not see them, it was evident that she wore anklets, because they made a seductive *jhin-jhin-tin-jhintin-jhin* sound as she shifted her weight from one foot to another. Her complexion had the soft hue of sandalwood, as indeed did the cloud of fragrance that surrounded her. *Jhin-jhin-tin . . .* Rama heard. It wasn't the bird song he must have thought as he whirled around. He blinked hard and gasped. In that nanosecond he was mesmerized by the apparition that he saw. *Jhin-tin-jhin-jhin*, she approached him. 'I'm Kamakanchini, noble warrior,' Soorpanakha uttered breathlessly, as she looked at Rama from head to toe. Rama understood and quickly said: 'Fair lady, what brings you to these dark forest regions, alone and unescorted?' That was polite code for: 'If you were a real lady of nobility, you would not be in the forest dressed for dinner for the robbers and wild animals. Could you be a demon?' Soorpanakha, underneath her disguise as Kamakanchini, realized that Rama was not just a beautiful boy but was perceptive as well. In spite of knowing who she might be, he was courteous, and that made her pant for him even more. She archly responded to his spoken enquiry: 'Ah! I must proffer my welcome to you, noble warrior, as you have entered this realm, all of which I own. Because of your good looks and your breeding, I have forgiven you for entering without my royal permission. But let me be brief. You are now mine. So, marry me and I will give you—'

She was interrupted by Rama's smile. It went through her heart like lightning. Then she was struck with agony. Sita approached Rama to take a closer look at the mesmerizing beauty. Sita was enchanted. But Soorpanakha, seeing Sita, grew so jealous, she feared her disguise of Kamakanchini might wear off. She struggled within herself to see the love between Rama and Sita as he gently drew Sita with his arm around her shoulder, his hand firmly folding her in by his side. Kamakanchini went on regardless: 'When you marry me you will have armies, navies, elephants, 1200 courtesans. You will be held as the most powerful man across terrestrial and extraterrestrial realms, as I will declare it so. Now, cast away this slip of a servant girl and be the man who you are!'

'Thank you for your kind offer. This is my beloved wife, Sita. So you must accept my refusal,' Rama said with courtly amusement, 'however I have . . .'

At this point, Lakshmana leapt down from his perch as he could see the demonic armour building up beneath Shoorpanakha's Kamakanchini. 'Beware Rama! This is a demon disguised. Let us not entertain her any further!'

'Hah! How afraid you mortals are when your senses are seduced by my beauty. Hmm! As his brother, you too have something to recommend in the way of appeal. So, why not marry me? I'll offer the same dowry, but as it is your brother I really want, let's just make it a family affair shall we!'

This was the perfect bait. Lakshmana was incensed: 'How dare you!' he tried to control his anger. He was, in fact, fidgeting with rage even as Rama was signalling him not to take the offensive.

'Of all magical wonders! Look at you, you've got the shakes!' *Jhin-tin-jhin-jhin* she came closer, 'when was the last time you saw your woman? I've really tickled your fancy hmm!' and she touched Lakshmana. As if a leopard had leapt out, Lakshmana seized his custom-made sword and chopped off Shoorpanakha's nose and ears, as she came into her true form. Sita only now understood the power of a demon rakshasa's illusion. Kamakanchini was so convincing, and somehow Rama could see through it.

Soorpanakha wailed as she saw the blood streaming and screamed: 'You will regret this! I will not forget! You will suffer for this!' In her agony, she stomped and made the whole of Panchavati shake. Trees snapped and the earth cracked. Then she flew out of the forest, across the ocean and landed with a great big thump in the court of her darling brother Ravana.

He was holding a regal audience with his architects who had come up with sustainable futuristic designs of illusory palaces armed with missiles that could not be seen.

Thhhhawunkh! She landed. Magicians, wizards, architects and generals, were flung out of their seats as they saw a river of blood preceding the mutilated figure of Soorpanakha clutching her face. 'Rrravannaaaaaaaaaaaaaa! See my agony! I was going to get Sita for you as a gift. But those two mortals bewitched by my beauty as Kamakanchini raped me! Awwhhhh . . . booohuwwwhuuw!' She bawled and wailed. Had she been human, she would have had tears streaming from her eyes and would have blown her nose like a trumpet. Alas! She was neither a human, nor had she a nose to speak of. Her performance was heart-rending just as well. After all, she had been rejected in love. Hearing the name of Sita, Ravana sat bolt upright on his throne. His twenty eyes from his five heads on either side focused on the one single image of Sita on her wedding day. 'My dearest sister,' he was able to hear himself say over his heart pounding loudly, now that an old flame of love had been reignited. 'How distressed you are! Tell me *who* has done this to you? I will deal with them in my Imperial Person and return the dignity that belongs to you, and our race of proud and victorious rakshasas!'

'It has worked,' thought Soorpanakha, 'Ravana will seek Sita.' Once Sita was off the scene, she knew, no one would stand in her way of conquering Rama's sole attention. 'Aaaaahunww! Oh, Your Imperial Magnitude of a brother, beware. Those two mortals are treacherous. I know their ways. Once you have got Sita, give them to me and I will design many intricate tortures to make them pay for what they have done to me, to you, to our great rakshasa race!' She received a thumping applause and a standing ovation as now the entire rakshasa race had been included in her personal injury. Both brother and sister knew that they had a personal stake in this and needed to sway the assembly in their favour to achieve their ends; Ravana wanted Sita at any price, and Soorpanakha was bewitched by Rama.

That night when the moon was shining over Ravana's exquisite palace, and a warm breeze was blowing from the sea into his apartment, he sat alone in the dark save for the moonbeams. He firmly clasped the chalice of wine and as he lifted it to his lips, he whispered: 'Oh! Sita, how long your footsteps have created maps of desire in my heart. I thought I had forgotten you. But no, you are real. I see you here. I can make hundreds of you. I am an imperial illusionist. But you are the only one; I must have the real thing.' He heard footsteps, 'Ah, Vibhishana! Brother, what makes you come to my humble abode, eh?'

'Ravana, I know your thoughts. Put them away for ever. This is one game that will tie itself around your neck and drown you. Think of all you have done for us rakshasas. You have acquired the vision of Shiva, you are given every object of power, and yet you choose to pursue Sita. Remember she is another man's wife. Not just an ordinary man. She is Rama's.'

'How dare you! Rama is overly celebrated because of his youth. He only possesses conventional good looks and he has had years of indulgent luxury to cultivate manners. What does he know about hardship? He does not deserve Sita. She is born of the spirit of fire. As we rakshasa are. I am rightfully returning her to the realm where she belongs. Can you not see the justice in that?'

'Brother, you know you cannot be defeated in arguments. But beware that you convince yourself of your inflated logic. It is not just you that is at stake, it is our entire race.'

Ravana gulped his wine. His brother Vibhishana was the only one who could speak the truth to him. A tear found its way down his cheek. 'Oh Vibhishana, how this heart aches. How do humans suffer this pain? Is it just our physical looks they reject? Why do we, when we think of those tender feelings become like them?"

'Ravana, you are such a generous being. Please, banish the thought of Sita, and let the world learn from rakshasas, that there are as many kinds of love as beings, and it runs deeper than the skin.'

11

The Golden Deer

Ravana took Vibhishana's advice and banished the thought
of Sita. Instead, he engaged himself in his aviation plans.
His chief aerospace marshal had been designing a chariot.
Ravana sought him out. 'Add wings,' he said.

* * *

'But we can communicate by air, we don't need wings. It'll
ruin the design balance of the craft,' said Indrajit.

'The hell I care about design balance. I want the thing
to have wings!'

'But why? The whole point of this research experiment
is to see if we can detect invaders in our airspace while we
are travelling on the ground and exterminate them!'

'Indrajit, this is not an academic experiment. I don't invest in something set up to fail in the name of the advancement of research. I want it to fly with *me* in it!'

The furrows on Indrajit's face collapsed out of sheer disbelief. But he knew Ravana meant it. 'Where, your Imperial Highness?' he asked gingerly. 'Above Lanka, across the ocean into the forests.'

'When, your Imperial, most venerated Highness?'

'Tomorrow, this very moment,' announced Ravana.

Indrajit's muscles across his face, shoulder and hand holding the stylus over the blueprints of the design twitched, and spasmed.

He had always dreamed of making something permanent in the history of aviation technology that could be reconstructed by future civilizations and marvelled at. In fact, had things gone according to his dream plan, we in the twenty-first century would be celebrating him as the father of the radar. But now, Indrajit had to resort to the rakshasa means of creating magic, conjuring the illusion of an aircraft that would fly its 20 tonnes in the air, across the ocean, into the forest as Ravana desired. But the price of that was that it would be an illusion, a trick of the imagination and no designs could be drawn or left behind for posterity. He steadied himself and grabbed all the scrolls of designs and bowing low to Ravana, the rakshasa emperor, weakly walked away.

The next morning at the same time as the day before, gleaming in Ravana's palace garden that stretched many acres towards the sea was such a chariot with wings.

Ravana had insisted that there should not be any fanfare. So he boarded the craft, and as Indrajit gave him the signal, the *vimanpakshi* as it was known flew into the sky with Ravana steering it westwards towards south-eastern India. It gave him a greater sense of power and he knew his prize wasn't far. 'After all,' he convinced himself, 'I did take heed of Vibhishana's advice while I was in my kingdom. I banished the thought of Sita. Now that I am away, things can be different.'

By about midday, he had steered the vimanpakshi into a forest. He received electromagnetic signals informing him of where his uncle Maricha was. But when he landed, he discovered that Maricha was sitting in the lotus posture of meditation and looked pale, almost holy! What a shock for Ravana that a distinguished royal rakshasa should defect to holiness.

'Maricha!' Ravana thundered, 'I want *you* to become a golden deer!' Poor Maricha levitated and crashed with this preposterous command. He had gone deaf having heard Rama's bow twang all those years ago in the Dandaka forest. His sight had become dim as having shut his eyes after the devastating sight of his mother Taraka being killed by Rama, he had been blinded by the intense vision of the light that Rama returned to that forest. Maricha had kept his eyes closed in meditation for a long time. He had been shell-shocked by what Rama had achieved.

'A golden deer? Why?' he managed to stutter.

'Because I want you to distract Rama.'

'What! Are you mad?' he retaliated energetically.

'Uncle, I'm asking you in the most civil manner known to me. You *must* become a golden deer. What's the matter with you? You used to teach us all as children and youths that one must always keep in touch with the tricks and power of illusion. It plays upon the mind like a drug. And after a while, one cannot see the truth for a lie. And now, look at you! You've just been sitting and concentrating on one thing and you're half yourself. Come on! Let the blood of the rakshasa race flow in your veins once more. When you are with me there is nothing to fear. You will never die; you will have immortality!'

Maricha trembled again at the name of Rama.

Fundamentally, Maricha knew his death was near. He had not been true to his rakshasa need of creating illusions for the last twelve-odd years. He had genuinely begun to see the treachery of rakshasa logic. He also had no inclination to harm humans. These were not only treasonous by rakshasa codes but negated the very being of their darkness. This, in rakshasa ethics, was morally corrupt. Maricha knew his time had come.

'Uncle! Can you hear me through that haze of meditation? If you do not obey my command, I will cut you in a thousand pieces and tie your spirit to a tree!'

Ugh! The worst possible punishment. Being cut up in pieces wouldn't hurt because as an old master at illusion, he would not suffer the pain. But having the spirit tied to a tree would mean no wandering, just locked in one place feeling all the things the tree would feel as others resting in its shade, lovers canoodling, robbers digging their treasure at the roots and then growing rowdy after drinking illicit liquor, assassins making plans, artists of black magic making corpses speak and all the time staying awake!

Maricha knew he would be killed either way. But he had a choice: by whom he wished to be killed.

The next day, it was late afternoon. As it was nearing the monsoon, the peacocks made their presence felt. The lapis lazuli blue of their bodies and the aquamarine green of their tails cascaded like bowers when they perched on trees. Rama wondered what might happen if he created the sound of rolling thunder with his bowstring, announcing the rain. Would it make them dance, unfurling all those beautiful eyes on their tails? That would entertain Sita. Just as he was strumming the bowstring, Sita was stringing samantha flowers along a strip of plantain leaf pith, humming:

> First the cruel blow,
> Stretched on a dulcimer of
> Arrows
> I screamed in silence.
> What did my Love do to deserve this?
> We have walked with heaving hearts,
> Our clenched fists pummeling through the dark.
> The radiant samantha has lit my way,
> to find petals where crushed stones lay . . .

Suddenly, she looked up and saw a soft twinkling mist appear through the low branches and shrubs. The fragrance was that of incense. She nimbly stepped forward, finger to lip as if to hush the cacophony of the forest. Immediately her eyes sparkled and her lips broke into a smile: 'Oh Rama, look! It's a golden deer! Its spots are like gems and its fur shimmers like gold! Look how it flits like a firefly between the leaves. Rama, please, could I have this deer as a pet? We could return to Ayodhya with it to remind us of our days at Panchavati?!'

'Sweet Sita, no. Let it roam free. After all, it is a creature of the forest,' Rama said trying to coax her out of this unusual enthusiasm.

The sparkling mist encircled her and she spun around distraught. 'All these thirteen years I have never asked you for anything for myself. Just this once when I want this gift of a deer that would make me so happy, you crush my desire with your coolness! And now . . . and now, the deer has fled.'

Rama was startled. It was true. She never made a request of her own. He had always had the companionship of her and his brother, but for her, there was nothing of her own. 'Lakshmana! Take care of Sita! I'll return with the deer!' Swift as the wind, he ran after the deer with his bow and arrows.

As he followed the path of the deer, quick to catch the trail of fluttering leaves and the sound of its flying hooves, he must have run a fair mile, crossed the stream past a clearing, and ventured deep into a brooding grove, catching every now and again its shimmer of gold. 'This is insane; I'm following a golden deer to take back to Sita? Nonsense! We've been duped by a rakshasa. I must put an end to its treachery!' He crouched, aimed his arrow and Maricha could feel the shaft strike his ribs and pierce his heart. He would rather die at the hands of Rama. But as was his nature, even at the end of his days he was prone to treachery. Maricha's form of a golden deer fell to the ground, but he cried out in a voice that sounded exactly like Rama: 'Help! Sita, Lakshmana, save me, I'm dying.'

The cry carried through the forest and reached Sita. She trembled, wringing her hands abjectly. 'Lakshmana,' she pleaded. 'What made me so insane? How could I have driven my Rama to his death? Lakshmana, please go after your brother, bring him back safely, I beg you!' She was shaking with fear for what had become of Rama, anger at herself, desperation at the distance that Lakshmana would have to travel, and confusion at feeling so volatile. It didn't help that Lakshmana continued standing with his arms folded resting on his waist and smiling at the sight of Sita. 'Sita, do you think Rama would have been duped by that apparition you saw? It is a demon disguised and Rama has shot it. He will return. C'mon, Sita, we are not talking about some ordinary warrior?! We are talking about Rama. I was there when he demolished Tataka and her son at Dandaka. He is swift to strike, like lightning. Calm yourself.'

But she kept wringing her hands. Her chest felt tight, her stomach in knots, and her right eye was twitching—an omen of unfortunate events to follow.

Lakshmana had never seen the bright-eyed and courageous Sita so distraught. She seemed to be seized by a momentary web of terror. He extended his arm and with a smile of reassurance said, 'Relax, it'll be ok. I'm telling you.'

'How dare you!' She shot back at him. 'Is this the moment you choose to make advances at me? When my Rama is dying? What a serpent you are!'

Lakshmana could not believe what had possessed her.

'Sita! Terror has cast a spell on you. Your words are stung with poison.' He cupped his hands over his ears. 'Alright! I will go against my will and duty. My beloved Rama told me to stay by you and protect you from the wild beasts. I will go and return with him and then you will see that my reassurances were not hollow words.' He was in such pain by her accusation. His eyes streaming with tears, and short of breath, he managed to draw out a sachet of powdered camphor and said, 'Stay still. I will draw this circle around you to keep you from further harm, possibly even from rakshasas . . .' He then ran to fetch his bow in pursuit of Rama.

Sita sobbed as she realized how much she had hurt him. What had come over her? Was it that time of the month? She had never felt so possessed by some desperation to break away from all the protection she had known so far, its sweetness and harmony. 'O Rama,' she whispered, 'return to me safe, my love will balm you. Why . . . oh why was I bewitched by that golden deer?'

She looked so tender. Her cheeks wet with tears, her hair dishevelled, her whole body poised with concentration on the object of her love.

Someone was watching her intently. From the undergrowth, Ravana gazed at Sita's beauty. He stroked his moustache with triumph. Maricha's sterling performance would go down in the chronicles of rakshasa ancestry as a master of illusion. Not only that, but what a magnificent display of disharmony he had created! Sita was bewitched, Rama left in confusion, and Lakshmana followed. And now Sita was left alone. Ravana's strategy had worked. In his delight, he stumbled, and this rustled the leaves. Sita whirled around, having regained herself. 'Who's there?' she asked defiantly. Ravana was quick; he appeared to her as an old and lame traveller with tattered satchels containing herbs and barks. A sort of wandering First-Aid man. 'What on earth are you doing wandering through this forest alone and in your condition?' she asked with some concern. 'Bhikshaam Devi! Would you be so kind as to give this poor soul some water,' he said feigning fatigue. She ran into the hut and brought out a pitcher of water, and standing in the middle of Lakshmana's circle, gestured to the old traveller to come and get the water. But Ravana knew the spell of Lakshmana's *rekha*. It was potent with positive energy and infused with lasers that would diminish his powers. So he pretended to hobble and put out his cupped hands like a spout to receive the water she poured from the pitcher.

The staff that he used as a crutch dropped, and he fell farther away from Lakshmana's rekha. 'I can't step out of this Rekha,' she said. He could detect her compassion. 'I understand dear lady,' he said and stretched his frail body close enough to the circle. As she knelt and caringly poured the water into his hands, he couldn't resist being transfixed by her loveliness again. 'I'm very lucky that my crumpled body can wander freely through these dangerous forests as I and my kind are protected by that fierce and magnificent Emperor Ravana.'

'What! Don't you dare utter his name here! Protection is one thing, but by devious and corrupt means is unacceptable!' said Sita incensed. Ravana loved her even more for this. 'The truly magnificent king is one who shows compassion to all beings and creatures, friends and enemies alike. That title of magnificence rests naturally on my beloved Rama,' she said with affirmative sweetness.

'Aarrrrrrrgh! That wretched RAMA again! I'll teach these two a lesson!' thought Ravana. He was also desperate to get out of here because he feared that his jealousy, like Soorpanakha's, would turn to rage and that would tear away his disguise of frailness.

'Dear virtuous lady, my arms ache. Please could you just lean the pitcher over a little,' he said and as she did so, her hands holding the pitcher were now well out of the rekha. Ravana continued confidently, 'Well might you think that Rama deserves the title of king. Your devotion to him is admirable as a wife, particularly in times such as these. But I hear he is in exile. What good is a king if he is roaming around like a wild beast in the forest, while one like Ravana sits on a throne and actually gets on with the business of ruling his subjects and expanding his kingdom?'

No one can tell what really happened. Did Sita raise her hand to wave aside what he said, or did she want to strike him? Ravana leapt up and reached for the outstretched hand and dragged her out of Lakshmana's rekha. He shook off his illusion as the frail mendicant. Sita was now on her knees, shocked and speechless. Ravana stood with his ten resplendent heads, all eyes looking at her. 'Silly woman, it'll teach you that wiliness is more useful than dumb loyalty!'

'How dare you!' Sita growled.

To Ravana, Sita looked even more ravishing. He whistled for his illusory vimanpakshi with one of his ten mouths, while he dragged Sita along the ground. She clung to it, crying bitterly, 'O Prithvi, my mother! Don't let me go! This rakshasa is taking me into the air! O mother, just bury me in your depths!' Ravana knew what Sita herself did not know; if she asked, all the elements of the planet would come to her aid. He was powerless against a woman. But he would not let her know that. So he lifted her from the ground and cast her on his shoulder as he strode into his aerial chariot, triumphant as he steered it through the air. At last, he had Sita. This was the ultimate conquest across time and space; it was the grandest trophy of Ravana's heart.

Kanda V

12

In Search of Sita

Lakshmana was running faster than a cheetah. If you had seen him, you'd say he was running away from himself. 'What do I tell Rama? If I return to Sita, she will . . . Oh! The terror of the fire in her eyes!' There were endless questions flitting through his mind.

Suddenly his foot gave way and was caught in a python-like grip. 'Lakshmana!' It was Rama, who had thought the intruder might be another rakshasa come to retrieve Maricha as the golden deer and take it down to the realm of the rakshasas. Maricha's face was twisted at death, but carried a malicious smile as if to say he had seen what was worthwhile in his last moments. Had he achieved what he wanted by meeting his end at the hands of an honest man? Or, was it that he had finally tricked Rama for murdering his mother in the Dandaka forest some years ago? It really depends on which way we view the world.

'I knew you would be alright! Let's return as soon as we can.' Lakshmana's relief was intense.

'You mean you left Sita on her own?'

'I . . . I don't know wha . . . I can't explain. But I left her safe in the *Lakshmanrekha*.'

Rama was not happy. His heart was pounding at the inextricable turn of events. 'You've done what you knew best. Hurry, we must hurry.'

They had barely started running when they were deluged by waves of anxious calls in the forest. There was a lot of screaming from birds and monkeys. They were sending warning signals of danger that lay in the direction Rama and Lakshmana were heading. The sun was going to set, and normally there would be a frenzy of activity before birds nested, but this wasn't that. There was a traffic jam too and the reason was that the elephants from a neighbouring forest had decided to move into Panchavati in search of more water and also to escape from trappers. Some were being trapped to be tamed as working elephants. While the pursuit of the golden deer expedition had begun earlier that afternoon, this traffic jam had occurred at the close of daylight due to a tiger attacking one of the female elephants and snatching a baby elephant. In the fading light, Rama and Lakshmana crawled between pillars of elephant legs and tails desperately hoping they could get back to their huts in time as Sita would be worried sick. That was all Rama thought about. What he would tell Sita. 'The golden deer was a new brand of rakshasa. Devious and menacing. Coming between us. Never, never, NEVER will we ever let anything come between us. Ever again.' His heart kept repeating this like a mantra, part affirming part despairing for the worst.

He could feel Sita's heartbeat echo with his words. Strangely, this was the first time during the thirteen years of exile that they had been parted from each other over an adventure. All he focused on was the story he would tell her when he saw her, waiting on the porch, for him.

Lakshmana was the first to reach the dwelling. He stopped, realising Sita would want to see Rama first.

Rama could see the Lakshmanrekha and then the broken pitcher lying on the earth. The water now left a shadow of dampness.

'Sita!' He called out. No answer. He hoped this was a game. 'She may have . . .' Then both brothers called her name as they searched and searched for hours.

When all the animals had hushed and settled for the night, Rama wept, and wept. Lakshmana could not forgive himself and would have put an end to his life if Rama's need for comfort had not been greater than his own.

Rama was inconsolable. 'I have never seen her upset. She was upset when I left. If only that had been a real deer I could have brought back for her . . . I would see her smile again. Oh Lakshmana, what is this thing called heart? Mine is given to Sita, why does it ache so much in my own body!' What could Lakshmana say? In the next instant Rama would say, 'Come on. Let's go this very instant and uproot all the trees and search among every herd of animals, where Sita is hidden,' and Lakshmana had to restrain him. In another instant, Rama would just sit and stare into the dark, motionless, almost without breathing, that Lakshmana almost took him for dead. They both grieved not knowing whether she was alive, carried away by a beast, or dead. They were relentless in their search. What had become of Sita?

At the close of day, when it was natural for the sun to set, Ravana's golden vimanpakshi, a flying chariot was blazing like a hundred suns. Its wheels were tearing away from gravity the way Sita's heart was being wrenched from all that she knew as her home since the day she married Rama. 'Oh, you creatures of the forest, I know now how it feels when a playful boy's catapult dislodges a nest of birds; or music betrays the snake to its charmer for his trade; or when the traveller's cooking fire wreaks havoc in the jungle. I am alone and afraid. How could one moment change the current of my life? Where are you, Rama? You creatures, who cannot speak my words, hear my anguish; tell Rama and Lakshmana how I've been taken against my will by sheer deceit!' As all these thoughts and feelings were welling up inside her, like a river breaking its banks, words remained unspoken. Suddenly, she witnessed the most spectacular sight. It was as if her thoughts had sent a signal for help, and at last, it was there in front of her.

A giant eagle with wings like vast ocean waves swooped in front of Ravana's vimanpakshi. 'Get out you irritating blimp of a fly!' cursed Ravana. 'How dare you obstruct my imperial path?'

'Ravana, I am Jatayu, Father of the Skies! I have come to rescue Sita. Her heart and soul are bound with Rama. You cannot take another man's wife. This is a crime and an invasion! She has *no* feelings for you . . .'

'How dare, how dare!' Ravana exploded and conjuring up a fire sword, he swung this way and that, from left to right and chopped off both of Jatayu's wings. The sky was splashed with red as the blood spurted from Jatayu's tumbling body; his screeching at this unimaginable loss of control, otherwise so natural to airborne creatures, was deafening.

This unforgivable violation of airspace had been perpetrated by disrupting the otherwise harmonious coexistence of human and avian species until this moment in evolutionary history. It spread terror.

Deep within Infinity, Brahma felt a new tide turn in His creation. There was a tsunami shift in the moral order of the world. Shiva was transfixed in working out an abstract theorem of the nature of cause and effect. But, where was Vishnu, the preserver and lover of the value of life?

Deep in his unconscious, Rama stirred. Getting Sita back was his sole, and immediate purpose for living. But deep down he knew that the value of life itself was at stake. If he did not do something now, a light would be extinguished, and the whole of humanity and its civilization would succumb to megalomania and be drowned in this brutish darkness of terror.

Rama and Lakshmana were continuing their search in the forest, when suddenly they saw what looked like a heap of feathers. As they approached, it seemed to be croaking: 'S-i-s-s-s-i-t-a.' Rama tried to untangle the heap of feathers, sticky with blood. It was Jatayu. 'Sons of Dasaratha, you have come,' he croaked. The breath in his body was thinning. But he saw Rama.

'How, oh how . . .' cried Rama.

'Ravana . . .' Jatayu swallowed.

'Which way?' Rama and Lakshmana asked. But Jatayu's eyes glazed over as he lost consciousness and entered the realm of death. 'Brave and noble bird,' wept Rama, 'how much you suffered to rescue Sita! Look at these gashes on your magnificent body! How my sweet Sita must be tortured by that tyrant! And where on earth was I!' His sorrow was a raw wound; his lament like a wolf baying for the loss of its hunted companion.

In the darkness of the forest, someone had caught sight of Rama. He was perched high on a tree. Ordinarily, he was described as a monkey. His name was Hanuman. He had special qualities that made the hue of his fur shine. He was on a secret mission for his army led by Sugriva, to check for spies in the forest. Of course, Rama and Lakshmana looked like prime suspects; warriors, newcomers to the forest. But when Hanuman overheard the name 'Sita' in their conversation, he realized their sorrow.

Rama and Lakshmana were suddenly sprayed with seeds and had hardly any time to react before they heard a 'H-h-hello!' from behind. Whirling around, they found no one. As they faced each other in puzzlement, through the corner of their eyes, they saw a face peering quite low from a tree trunk. They faced him, and Hanuman bowed low. He took a glimpse at Rama and intuitively knew he was in the presence of someone who was gentle, but whose anger had been spurred by grief. Hanuman bowed low, 'I couldn't help overhearing your conversation. I heard the name . . .'

'Sita!' Rama's eyes lit up. 'You've seen her? Even if you had never set eyes on her before, you would know who she is . . .'

'It is true. There was a lady whose likeness in nobility had not been encountered. I only caught a glimpse of what looked like a plumed chariot in the time you mention when she went missing. It seemed as if it blotted out the sun! Count on me as your ally and we will seek her. But first, you must come and be hosted by my exiled King Sugriva, and then we will make plans when you are refreshed.'

Rama and Lakshmana had lived in the forest these many years, always on guard. On meeting Hanuman, they felt a sense of homecoming and trust, like meeting a friend from childhood.

Rama was surprised, but willing to have a friend the likes of which he had never had before. Hanuman in his monkey form was gentle and you could tell he was modest about his immense strength.

Legend had it that he was the son of the God of Air, Vayu. One day he saw the sun and thought it was a great big fruit in the sky. He was always determined to work hard to get what he wanted. So he flew up to the sun, but Indra, the god of the heavens thought the sun would be stolen from the sky, so he cast his thunderbolt at Hanuman, and he was struck to the ground, lifeless. Vayu lifted Hanuman and with the gift of breath, brought him back to life again. Since then, Hanuman had a special gift. He could take one breath of air and become twenty times his size and fly through the sky. He could also take one breath of air and become tinier than the tiniest insect if he so wished. But Vayu had instructed him that this gift of air and life would only hold value if Hanuman used it in the function of good. How is one to know what's good from bad when one is so young? Vayu became his instructor over feelings and emotions and how they created different patterns of breathing. When angry, the breath is short, when morose, the breathing is almost still, when one exercises, it improves circulation, the breathing is well paced and the body energetic to do things. So, Hanuman is always associated with the energy of life.

Rama, with all his training in yoga, could see the way Hanuman walked and talked. His whole demeanour showed his strength and a deep sympathy for other beings.

At last, they reached a grove and saw very distinguished monkeys sitting in a circle. Each was introduced as a general and finally Sugriva, the exiled king. Hanuman was the chief minister. When Sugriva heard Rama's story, he listened with deep concern. He vowed to help in every way that he could, and offered the services of his generals and Hanuman who was closest to him. But he had one major obstacle. He was exiled by his brother Vali in this forest.

'What has brought this on?' asked Lakshmana.

Sugriva said, 'There is no greater bond than that of love between brothers. But once that is betrayed, there is no greater terror. Vali and I were called to defend the mountain by this forest, as Mayavi, a rakshasa had possessed it. We knew that there was only one entry that also functioned as an exit. So we thought the best strategy would be to steer the demon into the mountain. Vali was daring and told me to keep guard outside. He pursued the rakshasa inside and there was a raging battle with clubs, maces and stone. For a while, the screaming continued. Then there was silence. Then a stream of blood flowed out. Vali's broken club rolled out. I did not want to take a chance with Mayavi. The mountain entry–exit had to be blocked. Vali had said, "Wait here until I return." My generals, soldiers and I waited for twenty-eight months. There was not a stir. With all my strength, I rolled a boulder the size of a mountain to the entrance and blocked it as I assumed my beloved brother Vali had been martyred in saving us eternally from the rakshasa Mayavi. I grieved and returned to the court and was crowned king. After a few days, Vali stood outside the palace and vowed to kill me as he alleged that I betrayed him. I tried to explain, but it was of no use. He beat me up. Such a hammering in public! He seized the crown. Then, he forced my wife to marry him. I had to retreat to this mountain that has been called Matanga after a sage proclaimed that it would be the only safe place to take refuge from Vali's wrath. It is the only safe place on earth where all the other privileges he has received from the superpower gods are useless. Vali does not dare come

near here, as the sage's curse will make his skull explode
into fragments. Vali had engaged in combat with another
rakshasa named Dandubi, who appeared in the guise of a
buffalo. When Vali gored Dandubi to death and chucked
his carcass, it flew and landed on a spot in this mountain,
where Sage Matanga was performing a sacred rite. The
sage moved on, but he left his curse on Vali for making the
sacred ground impure.

'So Vali stays away but he sends his spies to check if I'm
alive. Time has passed without counting. I feel extremely
fortunate I have such loyal comrades who have helped me
heal quietly in this mountain forest.'

'Are you going to remain in exile, or has Vali marked a
time for it to end?'

'This is a fate worse than death. I know I am alive,
I have powerful allies, I still love Vali as a brother, but
trying to push past his misunderstanding is like hitting a
stone wall. He sends his spies to make sure I'm alive and
living. I do not want to give my life up, as I know what
will be inflicted on my comrades who are deemed traitors
by him.

'Now you know my story, please let me unburden your
grief. I saw your noble wife being wrenched away and no
power of the gods enabled us to rescue her from Ravana.
You are looking at me as if to enquire what proof have
I. Understandably. Here, Hanuman,' and Sugriva held out
his paw as Hanuman gave him a small bundle. It was a
fragment of Sita's sari. In it she had managed to tie a ring
that Rama had given her. 'She must have wanted us to

know she was overpowered,' said Lakshmana consolingly, as he remembered the time when Rama had the ring made especially for her. Sugriva added, 'The direction of the wind must have been south-east. At least we know where that deadly aircraft went. I am your ally and we vow that Sita will be by your side.'

Hanuman coughed gently. 'First, we must ensure that Vali is not a threat to Sugriva, and then we will be free to gather our armies and search for Sita.'

The next day was like any other day, except that it was different. Sugriva ran up the mountain on the edge of his usurped kingdom and began screaming, 'Vali, if you are not a coward, then don't hide!' Vali heard this, 'Hide! Hide! I'll tan his hide for being such a pest. Rascalbadwa! Who does he think he's calling a C O W A R D!!!!?' He stomped into his wife's apartments to get his lucky mace. Off he went and encountered Sugriva. They flung into combat with ferocity. All the myths around Vali's indomitable power were true. Sugriva was strong too, but he was losing out on stamina.

Rama and Lakshmana were hidden low among trees. Rama arched his arrow in his bow in an attempt to strike at Vali. But at that distance and with both of them flying using their tails, between branches it was difficult to tell who was who. Rama certainly did not want to strike Sugriva. Poor Sugriva had built high hopes of being rescued by Rama, but now he couldn't hold out much longer, and felt faint. 'Hah!' screamed Vali, 'Who's the coward, eh?' and rushed off to his palace.

When Sugriva came, he said, 'Rama, if I had known you were going to let me down in this way, I would never have called on Vali. You assured me . . .'

Rama was agonized by what Surgriva had undergone but appealed once again: 'Please give me another chance, Sugriva. I just could not make out who was who.'

'I've survived by the skin of my teeth. How can I trust you again?'

'Why don't you show how far you can strike an arrow?' said Hanuman. 'Vali was able to split that tree there.'

Rama was quick to pick up the challenge. He strung the arrow in his bow and shot it. The arrow whistled past and the bow string juddered with a sound so thunderous, all monkey generals, with their high-frequency hearing, had to swallow hard as they cupped their ears. The arrow was at such velocity, it tunnelled its way through the trunks of seven successive trees. Sugriva was reassured. Hanuman had built confidence on both sides. Lakshmana and he shared a little smile. They knew how important the bridge of diplomacy was in times of conflict, especially among trusted allies. 'I hope we can continue our friendship,' said Lakshmana.

'Sugriva, call Vali out again and let's settle this once and for all.'

'Call Vali out again!? Did you see how he was making meat balls and chutney out of me? Ohhhhh no! I thought you showed your amazing arrow-zinging-through-seven-fat-trees so you could do the whole grand thing yourself. Call Vali out again?! Am I crazy or something!' Sugriva's indignation made his broken cheekbone hurt even more. He was right. The cloud of despair was thick. Hanuman too knew that to mess around with Vali the first time around was dangerous, but the second time around would be fatal.

Something sparked in Rama. Even Lakshmana noticed a change in his person. 'I'm sick and tired of all of us being punished by tyrants. What is the use of us being goodie-goodie and never taking a stand or defending our position? How will virtue survive if it is beaten down by our own incompetence? Can you not see we are letting Vali and Ravana get away with terrorizing a normal way of life; the heart of our simple existence?' As he said this, deep within, Rama remembered the timely and subtle teachings of Sage Vashistha. It was taking effect. As a sixteen-year-old, when Rama had said to the sage who had been appointed by King Dasaratha as a mentor that he did not want the pomp and circumstance of a royal life, and that he would set off to the mountains as an ascetic and contemplate on Brahman, pure consciousness, Vashishtha who had introduced the concept to him gave him lessons on understanding that Brahman is everything; in a hut on a mountain, or in the palace or on the battlefield. But the balance of knowing when to act and for what purpose, making the right choice that will sustain life—that is the struggle; calling upon consciousness to be empowered when you feel powerless and how to practice it is the real lesson.

'You mean to beat them at their own game?' asked one of the generals.

'Are we no better than them then?' enquired another.

'But if we keep sitting on our backsides, we'll be flattened by both of them together!' concluded another who was waiting for action.

'I have a suggestion,' said Lakshmana who was also tired of this prevarication. Rama was right. Some action to uphold their rights had to be taken.

'Why not Sugriva wear a garland around his neck? That way Rama will tell the difference between the brothers.'

There was a grand applause of stamping and whooping.

The next morning, Sugriva was armed with new knowledge. He would fight against how he and his wife and kin had been wronged. He called Vali out at the city gate of Kishkindha. This time Vali was not outraged; he was amused and strutted to the palace ramparts. 'This exile has really cooked his brain. Look at him standing wearing that sissy garland and dancing before death.'

'Be careful,' warned Tara, Vali's wife. 'He must have some supernatural support. You beat him up yesterday, he can only return with confidence if something else is there. My spies tell me . . .'

'Exactly, he returned because I must have blown the sense out of his brains. Ha! Ha! Who can touch me? I have the blessings of the gods because I have been strong and loyal to my subjects!' and off he went.

Vali and Sugriva wanted to make short work of this fight. They butted heads, entwined tails, shrieked, leapt and parted to fling themselves at each other again. Rama waited for the moment and seeing it clearly, he shot Vali.

Vali staggered and seeing the arrow sticking out of his thick chest, pulled it out and read 'Rama' on the inscription.

His eyes bloodshot, he screamed, 'How could you be so devious, Rama? You know if you had asked for my help, I would help you against Ravana. Why did you not fight with me yourself?'

'Vali, you had all the privileges a brother could have in a loyal sibling. Yet you chose to believe the worst. Without consent or counsel, heady with power, you abducted Sugriva's wife, forced her to marry you and then exiled him. What justice is that?' Rama's words chimed with the truth of the matter.

Vali realized the deep bond between brothers; kinship and loyalty had been violated and he died with that understanding.

He was cremated, and Sugriva was marched with pomp to his former palace to be crowned king. He kept his promise to Rama that he would help in the search for Sita.

13

Promises, Promises

When people vow to do something, it becomes the single focus of their lives until it is completed. When someone makes a promise, it often involves at least one other person who anticipates the fulfilment of the vow undertaken. 'Losing faith in someone if they haven't kept their promise is the worst punishment,' said Rama as he watched the rains pour down in the forest, wiping out all tracks of their monkey comrades, Sugriva and Hanuman, who had returned to Kishkindha to get on with the coronation and stabilizing the kingdom. Rama and Lakshmana were in exile so they continued to stay in the forest.

The croaking frogs, lotuses stripped of their blossom and the dance of the peacocks had no charm for Rama anymore. Once, while sheltering under a tree, Rama looked at the red backs of the tiniest mites struggling to get a speck of dry food home amidst what was a trickle of water. But for the mite, it was like a huge ocean.

Lakshmana, sensing Rama's despair asked: 'The sun and moon have passed several cycles behind the dark rain clouds. The white cranes move swiftly, soon the *sharad* will be on us. What has happened to Sugriva? Maybe I should go and remind him of his promise?'

'You've read my very thought,' said Rama.

Sugriva had got ever so slightly carried away with feast after feast, day after day celebrating his long-awaited kingship and being reunited with his wife and son. But when Lakshmana went to visit him when the rains ceased, Sugriva said, 'I have not forgotten.' He, accompanied by his comrades, went to meet Rama in the forest.

Jambuvan, the general of the bears, was invited. Angada and Hanuman took the lead on behalf of the monkey generals. In front of a fire lit with a few dry branches, they took an oath that they would never doubt one another and have faith in their mission of seeking Sita. Then they sat down to figure out how.

'We know Ravana has taken her away, but where?' asked Jambuvan.

'I think we have to carry out a systematic search,' said Hanuman.

'But even if we do find her, how will she know who we are and who has sent us?' enquired another general.

'More importantly, how will you recognize her?'

Angada said, 'Hanuman, you should take the lead. You are gifted with powers that can see beyond what we can and can take us across the sea and sky.'

'That's true, Hanuman, I will miss your able advice, but I know only you will be able to cover the whole earth in your search and return with success.'

Rama had hoped that Sugriva would entrust Hanuman with leading the 'Search for Sita' campaign. For obvious reasons he could not say it first, as Hanuman and everyone else concerned were part of Sugriva's armies, and Rama never failed to remember he was an honoured guest. Making claims on the virtue of his own physical prowess and defeating Vali, would break a bond of friendship and military alliance based on trust.

Hanuman remembered his father Vayu's words: 'Use your powers that I bestow on you in the service of good, and you will triumph. Always discriminate between what is good for all, not just what is good for you. Don't seek what is instantly pleasurable. Test its endurance. Don't shun what might seem like hard work. It might offer the fruit of service as a reward. Above all, seek that which is truth. Smell it, touch it, taste it, hear it, speak it, see it and show the truth to others. It is your best friend.' When he saw Rama approach him, Hanuman knew what his father meant about serving what is good for all.

While the others were hurrahing about the first decision that had been taken, Rama drew Hanuman aside and putting his arm around his shoulder said, 'You will know Sita when you see her. The creepers of the forest were envious of her tresses that hang around her waist. Her feet are nimble, and her eyes speak with fire. The power of her words is great, however, few may pass her lips.' His eyes were welling up again.

'But how will she know I am your friend and servant?' said Hanuman who was deeply moved by the anguish of Rama.

Rama carefully removed the ring from his finger. 'Here, this will not fail to be a passport to her faith that help is at hand.' Sita had given it to him inscribed with her poem.

Hanuman leapt with delight, at being entrusted with such a precious task; of reuniting love and justice.

The schedules were set. Different generals took their forces in the direction they were familiar with. Hanuman, Jambuvan and Angada decided to go south. Everyone decided they would meet in thirty days' time, where the oath-taking fire was lit. The sun was now reappearing in the sky after a long and torrential monsoon. With a wave of hope surging in his heart, Rama watched Hanuman go.

14

In the Thick of It

The tumult of guards, soldiers, alarms and rakshasas created an inventive dance of chaos. Hanuman decided to sit down and eat a piece of fruit with one paw while with the other he itched himself like an ordinary monkey. But each time commanders from Ravana's police units came forward, he would throw a piece of rubble at them. Stretcher-bearers were running a relay carrying out the seriously injured.

Reports reached Ravana at his headquarters. 'Nonsense!' he barked. 'How can a monkey lead us on a merry dance!' The rakshasa nation was told to rise again. Cheerleading songs were sung and new rakshasa units replaced the injured. 'Indrajit, you are my hope and son, go and capture that monkey,' said Ravana with deep significance.

Indrajit watched from a tower over the exotic garden known as Ashokavan. He could see through his magic telescope a timid monkey creating havoc. So Indrajit took out a special weapon called Brahma Astra. He slung it in his bow and shot it at the monkey. Hanuman was immobilized.

Amidst the cheerleading songs was a great cry of 'GOAL!' Then the heftiest of rakshasas bound Hanuman and brought him to Ravana's palace.

'Great!' thought Hanuman. 'I can see the secret doorways, entrances and exits to this palace. Just what I wanted.'

'SPEAK!' demanded Ravana's speaker of the House of the Rakshasa Lords.

Hanuman replied calmly, 'I am a friend and envoy of Rama. I came on a mission to see where his wife Sita had been abducted and held hostage . . .'

'Lies, sheer monkey-tricking lies!' Ravana protested. 'Sita came on invitation and she is considering her future . . .'

Hanuman interjected swiftly as he knew from Sita's account in the Ashokavan a little while ago what she suffered. 'My message from my Master, Rama, is that you return his lawfully wedded wife Sita to him, and there will be peace, otherwise prepare yourself to face his wrath in a fight for what is right against might.'

'Let's kill him,' said Ravana impatiently.

'Brother! How can you do that? This is an envoy from another royal realm and if you violate the code of courtesy while interrogation, you will not have any power to negotiate when there is an intra-planetary crisis.'

Hanuman was surprised at this voice of lucid judgement and when he saw Vibhishana's face, he recognized him to be the rakshasa who gave him milk when he was prowling around as a cat.

Ravana had to take Vibhishana's advice into account as he was held in great esteem by all the rakshasas. He agreed and then suddenly his mood changed and he gave the command, 'Let's set fire to his tail just to see how he jumps!'

Hanuman stood. The rakshasa Special Forces Unit lunged at his tail with delight. 'This is public enemy number one. Torturing him is a great honour and will save the face of our rakshasa nation,' they thought in fundamentalist unison.

They grabbed its tail and started bandaging it with highly flammable material. They thought they would make a quick job of it. But the tail had a strange quality of heaviness and was slippery and would just dangle away from their grasp.

'How come it keeps getting longer as it gets heavier?' they thought as they heaved together.

The tail had, in fact, stretched to three and a quarter miles, the radius of the inner city of Ravana's kingdom.

The end of the tail was then doused in oil and set alight.

One small breath was all it took from Hanuman and he grew in size and burst through his shackles. The flames were licking the flammable material, which was soon blazing.

Intermittently, the rakshasas shouted, 'Hah! That'll teach this monkey!'

'See how pain and fear have made him leap . . .'

But Hanuman was flying now with his flaming tail, and, swooping over them like a trapeze artist, setting everything alight.

Sita heard the beams snap like wrestlers, knuckles as the fire took grip of everything within its path. She saw the sky ablaze. She prayed to Agni, her fire guardian, that Hanuman be unharmed. Strangely, Hanuman saw the flames receding from his tail, but growing fierce and intense over Lanka. 'Oh no! I've done it again! What has become of poor Sita!' He flew past Ashokavan and blew a cool stream of air over her so that she was untouched by the force of the fire. Seeing her wave back at him meant all was well and that she wished him a victorious mission.

In the dark, Hanuman flew even faster, and it was late by the time he reached the forest. Rama greeted him with fresh fruits and clear water. Hanuman knew the news Rama thirsted for. Rama would listen to an entire episode about Sita and the bodyguards. Then he would request Hanuman to repeat the exact words she said. Fortunately, Hanuman was attentive and had a good memory, so he was able to repeat verbatim what Sita had said. Rama knew this was true by the sheer cadence of the words, as he remembered how she used to speak. Rama knew that Hanuman was holding back from telling him how much Sita suffered; he could tell by the restraint in Sita's speech what she endured. His heart ached like a wound reopened.

His rage at Ravana took on strange proportions. He couldn't help himself from thinking; here was a powerful rakshasa king who called himself an emperor who subjugated everyone and everything, except his own illusions. 'What kind of example of a royal person is that to look up to and emulate?'

'Brother, our one course now is to save Sita,' said Lakshmana.

'Yes, Lakshmana. But that is not the only reason for confronting Ravana. We cannot live like worms and feed off the earth, we have minds, memory and culture; we must protect this earth not only from its natural disasters when we can and must strengthen its moral fibre. What good am I as man, husband, prince, or would-be-king to Sita if I did not live for an ideal?'

Hanuman and Lakshmana could only sense his pain, and strangely further his feeling of loss and abandon for Sita. Rama had learned how much Sita had changed in the course of these past few months living as a hostage, and in someone else's territory. It must have rankled.

Rama gathered his scattered emotions and thoughts for Sita and looked directly at Hanuman: Of course, the next question is a report of all the strategic positions of Lanka. Hanuman replied with a detailed account of other possibilities of entry into Lanka than the underwater cave he had been in. 'The only problem,' Lakshmana concluded, 'is that there is this vast bulk of ocean and how do we cross it?'

'And, do we have an army in the first place?' queried Rama.

Hanuman peeled off the last wadge of bandage from his tail carefully and said, 'An army can be arranged. I'll sort that out now.' Rama and Lakshmana thought he was going to send a messenger to inform Sugriva of his return and whereabouts. About an hour passed and Rama and

Lakshmana were a little concerned that Hanuman did not return to bid them farewell with his usual courtesy. He must have been exhausted, they concluded. But as they sat keeping watch, they heard a low humming sound that gradually grew louder in the night forest.

The glow worms winked, even the nightly drone of the cicada was submerged in this ocean of 'Hmmmmmm'. Then the first signs of the earth throbbing as the 'hmmm' grew closer. It seemed as if there was nowhere to hide or perch to detect where this was coming from. It seemed to be surrounding Rama and Lakshmana, and closing in on them.

Their eyes had been trained to be accustomed to see things in the dark. Suddenly it looked like the trunks of tall trees were approaching them as the Hmmmmmm was now like a spaceship ready to take off.

Rama and Lakshmana had no choice but to be crouched like stalking cheetahs, with their backs to each other so that they had the tight circle of space around them covered.

Suddenly, Rama saw a figure weaving between these moving tree trunks. 'Hanuman! What on earth!'

And then the earth jumped along with everything on it and the tree trunks stood still. Rama and Lakshmana were sprawling, clinging to tufts of foliage to steady themselves. Hanuman bowed low: 'Dearest Rama, I'm so sorry, sor . . . sorry. I didn't think you would be so startled. I just thought the best thing to do rather than tell you was to sort out an army. I might as well bring them here to show you!'

Lakshmana and Rama stood up, dusted themselves to look fairly leader-like to receive the army when it arrived.

Then smiling and bowing again Hanuman said: 'Err . . . and here they are.'

Rama and Lakshmana cupped their hands like binoculars to see clearly and then it hit them!

The trees were not trees! They were the legs of tall monkeys and their heads were as high as the tops of the tallest trees. Their eyes were like torches. The Hmmmmmm was them breathing and the throbbing and pounding of the earth was them walking in unity! And there was Hanuman looking so tiny in comparison, but what respect he commanded!

Lakshmana gulped several times and Rama with his good humour said, 'Well . . . Hanuman, you certainly have a way of rustling up surprises. This is hugely welcome.' All the monkeys laughed, and then Hanuman surrendered their command to Rama.

'Friends, my spirit and that of my brother embrace you. As you can see, our bodies are limited. We are humbled and privileged by your allegiance and in the trust you bestow on us. For this I am eternally grateful to my beloved friend and guide, Hanuman.

We now have a mission to accomplish. There is nothing straightforward about it. All we know is the destination and why. We do not know how we will get there. The obstacles are great. While all the pathways to Truth are one, it is about shifting the obstacles of our mind and spirit that make the journey arduous.

There are no quick fixes to life. We will face victories, and there will be corresponding defeats in the deaths we would have to pay with. I am not seeking war, so those of us who are thirsty for it, know that we may end in peace due to a diplomatic settlement. And for those of us who do not want war, we would have to be prepared to realize that a diplomatic settlement could not achieve the justice we requested. Our opponents are not our enemies in that they must be hated; we must remember that they think and act differently from us. Our main concern is the injury they cause the world over, and that is the fight for right against might.

All I can give you is my life that upholds a belief in justice, not only for me and those whom I love, but as a world order where we all act responsibly and for each other.'

Rama ended. It wasn't intended to be a speech, but it made the monkey army realize the kind of person that was leading them and understand why Hanuman would recommend him.

It started with one clap of thumping fist on chest and soon there was a thunderous applause not solely for the speech but as an oath of allegiance.

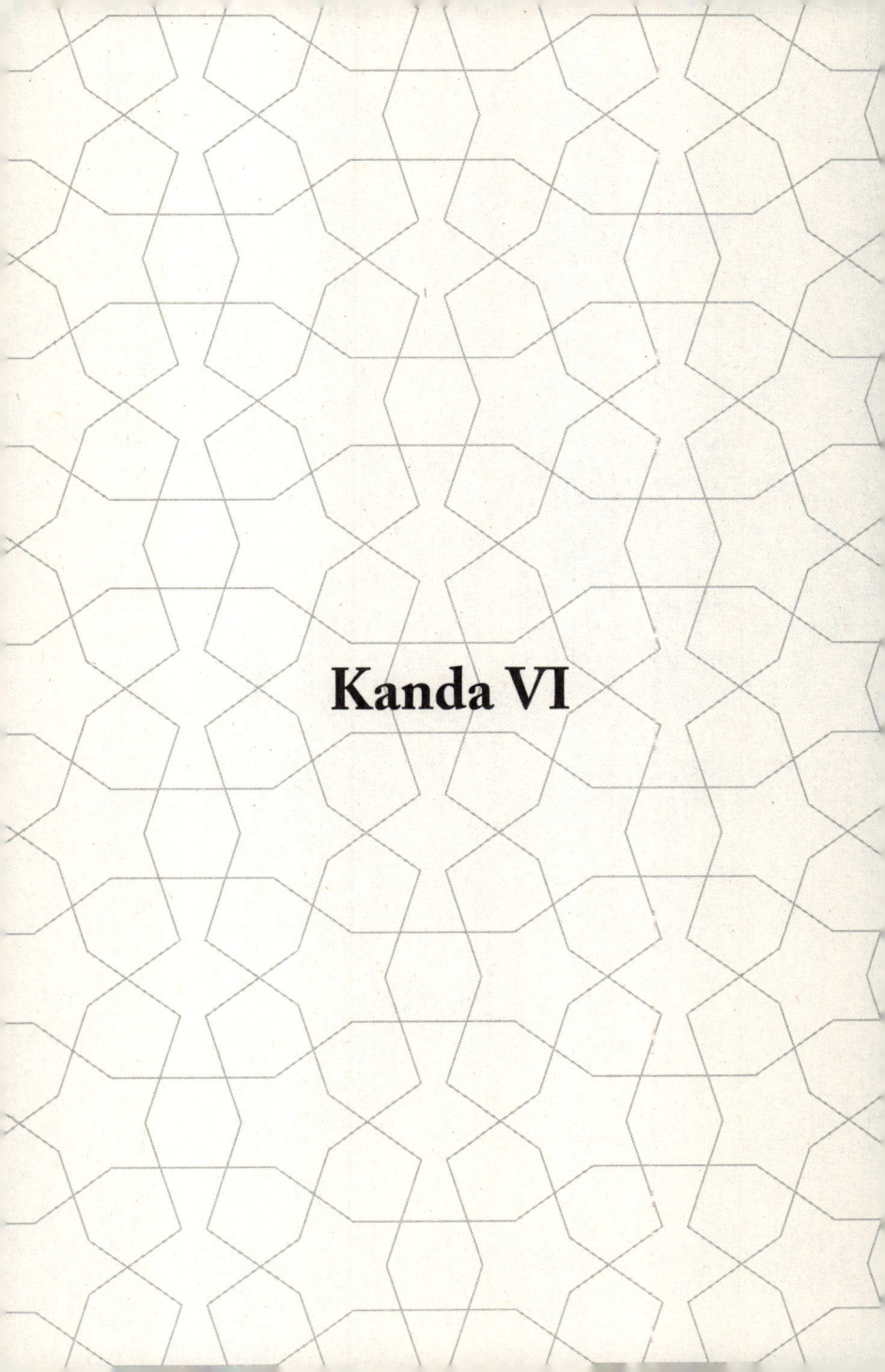

Kanda VI

15

Neither Here Nor There

Ravana watched the city he built from tiny grains of sea sand and wood blaze in the tyrannical fire. It blazed for days. The stench of decomposed rakshasas and burnt flesh barbecued on fallen wooden beams, made anyone who was alive and able retch.

A few of his ablest commanders, and his close advisers, were dead. Their bodies were unidentifiable, except for the jewellery that they had on, and even that was semi-melted. He felt their loss and it hurt. Ravana had always been alone and cast off. The sense of abandon always hovered around him like an omniscient bully. His only way to combat this feeling was to become angry and blame someone else for his painful loneliness.

He was furious that Hanuman had wreaked this havoc. He was angry at Vibhishana for intervening with the codes of diplomacy; he was livid that his forces couldn't handle the impact of this disaster. He was abusive to his public relations staff for constantly bringing him news of the death toll, and then in the same breath wanting his advice on how this debacle should be featured in the inter-terrestrial news forecasts that propagated the rakshasa way of living as being best.

Ravana had, a long time ago, known that enemies such as the gods of the heavens and the mortals as well as the gods of the underworld would be jealous of his endeavours and the success he had achieved. So, he had built an underground palace that was as lavish, and in fact much cooler than the one above ground.

The difference was that it was windowless and naturally dark, and all the lighting was artificial, made by lamps reflecting on polished shields, gems and gold. This did, however, affect people's moods if they spent a long time underground.

Ravana was in one of his rooms, alone. 'It's all because of her! That Sita!' he said fiercely. 'She is the cause of all this menace to my kingdom. If she had agreed to be my chief wife, all this would not have happened . . .' he trailed off. He heard anklets. One more sip of wine. 'Sita!'

The anklets and footsteps belonged to his chief wife, Mandodari. 'I came to see how you are.'

'You can see, can't you?'

'As your chief wife, my concern is for your welfare. It begins with taking account of some of the things you have done that have come to this state.'

'Blah! Blah! Blah! Nag, nag, nag! That's all I hear.'

'All I'm warning you about is: be careful of how you think of Sita.'

'Hah! After all this time ensuring she stays barely alive with your supervision of the food she eats, now the real jealousy surfaces!' Ravana exclaimed.

'If it was given for me to treat her as other, I might have felt jealous . . .'

The drink was getting a hold of Ravana and to repel it, he grew contemptuous. 'Oh! Stop speaking in these useless riddles.'

Mandodari continued cautiously: 'All I will say then is *don't* think of her as just anyone . . . just . . . someone else's wife.'

'I don't *believe* this! After so many years, you are preaching this to me!'

'No, Ravana, she is more than that, she is closer than you think, and must be looked upon as the farthest object of your desire.' The tears welled in her eyes, as her mouth dried of words.

How could Mandodari tell Ravana about the pot of blood and milk stolen from the holy man that she had drunk from and had made her pregnant? All those years ago, Vibhishana had rescued her then by taking the female infant a few hours after birth to a faraway place. If she told Ravana anything now, Vibhishana would definitely be killed. If she remained silent, a greater evil would be committed; by both, her husband in loving Sita, and Sita realizing the story surrounding her birth.

While this dilemma was twisting her stomach into knots, and making her head reel, she heard the wine goblet tottering on the polished floor, the cup a bleeding wound spilling the red remnant, and Ravana's footsteps receding into the hallway.

Ravana strode towards Ashokavan with one single aim. Nothing could stop him now. In her cell, Sita was looking out at the night sky. It had never darkened. The heat and light from the blaze made it look like a continuous sunset. It wasn't peaceful. There were constant explosions and the cries of the anguished could be heard all around. She could not disguise the fact that she was happy that at last there was contact with Rama. This was the first step towards his triumph, that he had agents who were loyal to him and believed in justice, not only for himself and Sita, but as establishing a moral order for the world. There was also a twinge of sadness because the rakshasas who were suffering now were all not wicked. They were merely in awe of Ravana's power. 'Rama will show the way,' she was thinking, as she sighed. The fragrance of sandalwood suddenly wafted in. She had always associated it with Rama, as she always prepared the paste for him before he bathed. In the dark cell, lit only by the flickering blaze, she saw him. It was Rama! 'Sita!' He whispered in his musical voice. 'I have come to take you away! Hurry!'

It was a nanosecond. Her body was tense, as she spun her head from the bars of the cell to the interior. She was ready to leap into his arms. She froze. His eyes had tears, his lips quivered as he saw the way she looked at him.

'But why have you come like a common thief?' she heard herself saying. 'Sssh! No one must know. Hurry!' and he stretched out his arm. Sita happened to remember the outstretched arm that once drew her out of the forest. Now she also caught sight of the right big toenail. It was so manicured. 'How . . . how d . . . dare you, disguise yourself as Rama!' Ravana was defeated. Only once had he seen Sita look at him longingly, and that was in his spell as Rama. 'Sita! Listen to me . . .' he tried. She vomited as she swooned to the ground. The bodyguards came running in and tried to revive her. Ravana withdrew, but now with a rapier sharp pain in his heart, that was flooding with the loneliness of the ultimate rejection.

16

Marking New Territories

Rama woke with a start in the middle of the night. His forehead was drenched in sweat. Lakshmana was instantly by his side. 'Are you not well, or was it a bad dream?'

Rama's heart was beating fast. 'It's Sita. She was walking through a tree-lined path. The trees were leafless. I couldn't see her clearly, there was a cloud of mist. She was calling me. I knew she was just ahead of me. But every time I caught sight of her, she was swallowed by some coil of smoke.'

'Our fears take the form of our loved ones to push us further into a course of action,' said Lakshmana thoughtfully.

'I just hope we haven't left it for too late,' said Rama and they both looked at each other as if the forbidden had been mentioned.

'It's two hours till light breaks in the sky. We must march to the beachhead before the birds start for the worms.'

Lakshmana summoned the army of monkeys and bears by blowing the call on the conch shell. It was unbelievable how so many hundreds of these huge creatures could be so lithe and swift as they awoke and started marching. Being vegetarians, there was plenty to snack on while on the move in the forest.

Hanuman carried Rama on his shoulders at times to give him a view of the entire following. Sugriva and his other commanders, each had divisions of monkey armies. Jambuvan and his comrades had divisions of bear armies.

Winding their way through the mountainous forest, firm-footed they marched. The whole earth was humming with a unity of purpose. To make up time, they soon started rolling down the hills, sometimes creating wheels with boulders and axles with fallen trees. Even though it was tumultuous and fun, they were as quick to come to order.

It must have barely been six-thirty in the morning, and the sun was already a golden orb in the sky. The sea was sparkling. The way it stretched out, they seemed to have come to land's end.

There was a big cheer till the very last animal soldier had made the journey's end. There was an uneasy hush as their faces took on the look of genuine perplexity, gazing at the vast expanse of water with absolutely no land in sight at the horizon. Some tried to test the water, but the dissolving sand beneath their feet alarmed them.

'How can one cross this bulk of water?' Some tried to measure the depth of the sea by walking into it, but they had barely stepped into it before the waves closed over their heads. These were no ordinary monkeys, they stood tall, with tree trunks for arms and legs. Their eyes were like beacons, red and menacing when ferocious, kind and wise when at peace, so deeply shelved beneath their eyebrows.

Rama bit his lip; he fought hard against the wave of defeat, particularly after last night's dream or premonition.

He decided to call on Varuna, the god of the waters. But there was no reply.

Before Sugriva or Hanuman could interpret his frown, Rama whipped out his arrow and shot it at the sea. Suddenly, the waters swirled and all the sea creatures at the seabed came out in the churning water. It created such commotion that Varuna thought it best to appear. He appeared in his fluid form, as blue as the water. His voice swam in their ears. He looked magnificent in his flowing robes of aquamarine, turquoise, sea-green grey and deep blue. His jewels were mostly pearls and other shellfish that caught the colours of the rainbow now that they were exposed to the sun. 'Rama, please, I beg you stop!' he pleaded.

'Well, then why didn't you come out when you were called? And that too with all the courtesy,' said Rama in a rage as he shot arrow after arrow into the water, trying to empty the sea in the process.

'You are injuring the entire sea world, and that will cause as much destruction to the balance of the earth as the moral disorder created by Ravana!' said Varuna.

The words struck their blow. Rama held his arrow arched tight in his bow.

'All I ask of you is that you part the sea. I need a direct pathway to Lanka to take our armies . . .'

'Before you raise your hopes, I have to say that I cannot do so.'

'But you're a god, aren't you? That too of the sea!' asked Rama, his heart crumbling inside him as his goal got even farther away.

'Yes, Rama, I am a god of the sea. But I am responsible for keeping its nature and protecting its cycles and beings. That is what keeps the balance on the earth, the climate and the tides. I cannot make exceptions. It is the nature of life that we have to find a way around it to achieve what we have to.'

There was a sound of intermittent thumping as many among the monkey and bear armies sat down in despair. Rama sighed.

Varuna said, 'But there is one thing I will help you with. Think ingeniously and create a bridge across these waters, and I will ensure that it is held afloat and will not sink with the armies marching on it.'

There was a hoot and cheer and Rama accepted Varuna's claim was a gift and uttered a soft song that calmed the sea animals that had been churned out of the ocean in his temporary rage.

The architecture and engineering division of Sugriva's army were put to work in working out how wide and long the bridge would be.

It was particularly challenging. Unlike other bridges that have been built in the world, this one could not have a foundation base at the other end which was Lanka, as that was now enemy territory. So the whole construction had to be done without being caught by rakshasa surveillance, and, of course, under Rama's leadership, nothing was to be done by the trick of illusion. No one was forced to do a task they did not want to do. It was done with the inspiration that united all capabilities.

Once the plans were approved, building materials were sought. Huge rocks from the mountainous coastguard were rolled down from the rear guard of the great monkey army. Then tall trees formed rails and scaffolds for the boulders that were set as a paving for the bridge.

The division of labour was according to ability with Hanuman overseeing the process. When the sea animals saw what was happening, they too decided to create favourable currents for the rocks and trees to get lodged in the seabed.

While all of nature, including crocodiles and whales, we are told, were helping in this historical event, the squirrel in the coastal forest looked on. 'I have no strength compared to these great and grand creatures . . .' she thought wistfully. Her eyesight, however, was extremely good. She watched the boulder and rocks being piled high. In spite of the trees offering a strong railing, she noticed there were crevices between the rocks where the sea could flow in and weaken the bridge. She scurried off to the beachhead in the heat and started carrying mouthfuls of sand to fill the crevices so it glued the rocks together. The other squirrels joined in too. Rama picked up the squirrel and held her in his palm, and with his index, middle and ring fingers stroked her to thank her for significant and timely help. He marvelled at how brave she was, ensuring she was never crushed under the feet of the others in carrying out her task. Ever since then, the squirrels in India have their three stripes along their backs to certify that they were Rama's bridge builders.

17

What Lies Beneath

Slowly, Lanka, the emerald island as it was known, began
to return to its promised state. The smoke had died down,
and the sea breeze from all directions had cleared the air
around the island swiftly.

It seemed as if the fog from the rakshasa mind had
also lifted. There were murmurs among the less fortunate
rakshasas that the kind of attack they had faced, must be
the sort that they inflicted on others. How devastating this
remorse was! Some argued about fighting back, and some
felt they should learn a few lessons from it.

Ravana's spies were about and reported this to him.
Ravana called an Extraordinary Emergency Council
meeting. 'So what do you propose we do?' he asked.

His chief counsellor of Lands, Properties and Estates
said, 'It is outrageous that we should suffer such a loss after
this fire. And there is no compensation we can claim from the

enemy because it wasn't an army. Just a monkey. What was our Security Service doing if the army was not capable of . . .' He broke off because the chief military commander butted in.

'Let us be objective. This is brought on by a history of a particular act. A man's wife was abducted, and he is now trying to attack us through his allies. If we wish to get compensation for our land and properties, then we must try and return what we have taken from them and claim compensation; really make them rebuild our kingdom with their sweat and blood. But were we to do that, it would be giving in to their devious ways of thinking. After all, monkeys were created for our amusement and food. Why not wage war the rakshasa way and have a war that will end all wars!' Ravana *did* like the sound of this. And there was wonderful music in the marching rhythm of the speech, that was accompanied by the clinking of the speaker's bracelets, earrings and rings.

'Am I allowed to speak?' came the voice of Vibhishana amidst the throng agreeing with the military commander when they saw Ravana beaming with approval.

Vibhishana had not slept for days as he was on a stretcher-bearer at times during the rescue mission, helped in organizing drinking water and food from his apartments while also making it available as a shelter for the injured. He was at the end of his tether, and his voice was not powerful. 'I think the military commander is right.' The assembled council said, 'Hear, Hear!'

Vibhishana continued. 'Only in that, we need to reflect on our offences. Let us return this lady to her husband. It

is the law of nature. With her unhappiness, we are doomed
because Rama is doing what is naturally right. Planning to
defeat us and our injustice. It is about cause and effect.'

Ravana was furious. 'My own brother, proclaiming
that we will be doomed. And by that slender boy without
a kingdom, called Rama! This is outrageous. You have
something to do with all of this. It was you who did not
want Hanuman killed. If I had not listened to you, Lanka
would not be in this state. *That* is cause and effect! I will no
longer tolerate your presence in my kingdom.'

That was all it took. Vibhishana knew his time was at
an end. How much more could he appeal when no one
wanted to listen to sense?

He withdrew from the council amidst the jeering
and booing, and with three of his minister friends, went
to Mandodari to bid her farewell. When they parted, she
knew Sita would remain a secret between them.

'If only we all did not fear him so much, we could
help him to see the truth that is going to be the final
ruin of him and the magnificent kingdom he built,' was
all Vibhishana said to the small group of trusted friends
before he got into a small boat with them and sailed
across the ocean.

Although the monsoon was officially over, there were
days when dark storm clouds would gather, and the rain
and wind would create havoc in the ocean. These were
difficult days for the bridge builders. They had, however,
made exceptional progress with the length of the bridge.
So, on a thunderous day when work of boulder-rolling

and tree-railing was in full swing, Sugriva's spies spotted a catamaran bobbing on the waves through a curtain of rain.

Sugriva instructed his guards that they be captured and presented before Rama. The four hostages were brought in front of the forest assembly consisting of Rama, Lakshmana, Hanuman, Jambuvan, Sugriva and some of the other military commanders of the monkey armies. Strangely, even in his shackles, one of the prisoners paid salutations to Rama by touching his feet. When his face was uncovered, Hanuman realized who this was. Some of the military commanders felt these prisoners should be hanged as they were from enemy territory and must have come to spy. Rama listened for quite a while and was wondering about the best way of acquiring information from them and dispense justice humanely. 'Hanuman, my trusted counsel, you've been very quiet. What are *your* thoughts?' asked Rama.

Hanuman took a deep breath and spoke. 'Forgive me for expressing myself thus. This is Vibhishana, rakshasa, brother of Ravana. Yes, he belongs to our enemy. But we have not considered his reasons for leaving them. Besides, whatever else you may think of him, remember that we judge him on how he protected the code of international law by ensuring that I, or any other, as an envoy of another kingdom, was not savagely killed. Placing himself in great danger, he persisted in making the assembly understand a code of ethics, where otherwise sheer barbarity would have ruled.

I may be biased, but I believe him to understand the value of good and how it needs be preserved. Let us not be taken by which race he belongs to, let us look deeply at what lies beneath the skin. With his friendship and trust, we will earn greater access to Lanka.'

Rama listened carefully and knew that Hanuman was not placing a recommendation before him. It was Hanuman's firm belief that Vibhishana should be one of the military commanders of Rama's army.

Rama welcomed Vibhishana as an exiled king of Lanka.

Vibhishana had made a very difficult decision when he had left the shores of his beloved Lanka. After years of feeling like an alien in his own country because he didn't follow the whims of the rakshasa crowd, or give in to Ravana's fancies just because he was an emperor, at last, he felt he had arrived at a place where he was befriended by kindred spirits, in Hanuman, in Rama, in Lakshmana and their armies.

Vibhishana's arrival was timely. While the bridge building was in its final phase, the next concern was what they would encounter in Lanka. But with Vibhishana's drawings of the exact locations of ammunition stores and secret passages to underground army reserves, Rama and his armies felt a new wave of courage. The high ideals of justice are important, but the actual lay of the land and the problems that might be encountered are what armies need to carry out their mission.

At last, the day arrived and the bridge was complete, stretching and snaking its way from India's south-eastern coast to just a half mile short of Lanka. This half mile gave the monkey and bear armies an advantage as it acted as a moat to their bridge and the rakshasas were terrified of crossing the sea. On the same day, Rama sent two envoys with a message: 'Lanka has suffered greatly. There is still time to end this grief in peace. Return the noble Sita, and we will withdraw in peace.'

When Ravana heard this, naturally he was furious. Why should he return Sita? That would be defeat. Not only that, were he to wage a full-scale war, that might impress her of how much he loved her, and then, his thoughts spiralled out of control. When he killed Rama, she would have nothing to pine for, and she would give in to him. Now, of course, in the central council, Vibhishana was not there to challenge and dissuade him from this delusion. The existing council members pandered to Ravana's ego with no thought to Lanka. 'How dare he suggest you return her? That too telling *you* what to do? Has he no manners or respect for age and experience and superiority?' they advised.

'Besides, if you were to return her, will it not be like we predicted? They would have the prize and still destroy Lanka!' These were analyses from the remaining councillors as well as his son, and Kumbhakaran his other brother who was a sloth-like rakshasa. When everyone's heart rages for war, what else can happen? Merely preparations for war.

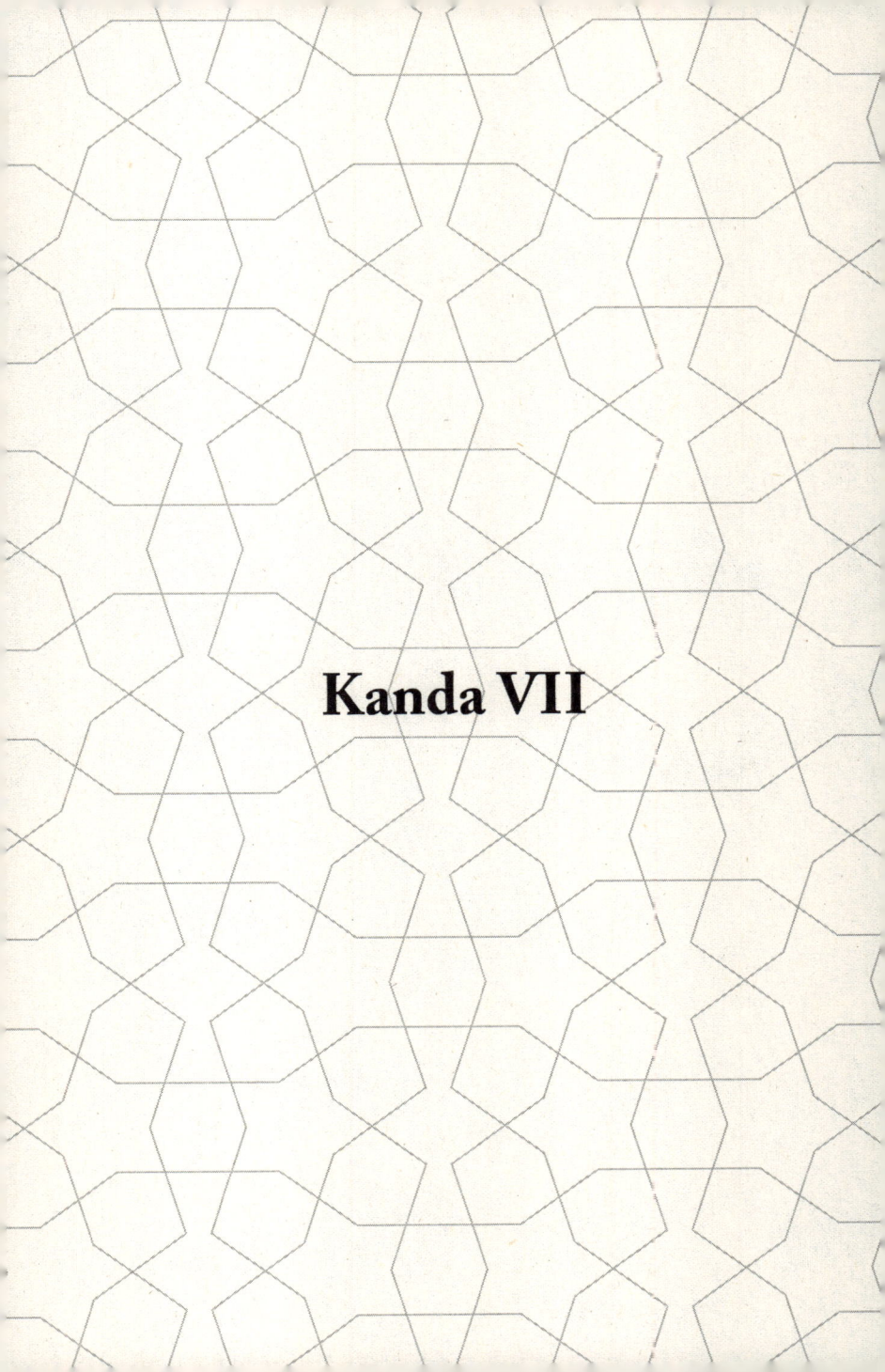

Kanda VII

18

The War to End All Wars

Rama's envoy had delivered the message in Ravana's court with all the respect due to a head of state, as per the diplomatic code. Ravana decided to send the two envoys back with a message. It wasn't with words. He had them strapped to a catapult that stretched from the watchtower of Lanka and then flung across the sea to the bridge. 'That'll teach that stripling to send me monkeys as messengers,' Ravana muttered as he saw their bodies flying out of the catapult.

The monkey envoys had suffered severe injuries by being hurtled on to the bridge. But they were in good spirits as they reported to Rama the chaos that reigned in the council, while everyone was pandering to Ravana's ego. 'He looked absent-minded,' they said. When the monkey and bear armies heard the report of the injustice and humiliation that these envoys suffered, their morale spiralled upward. They were ready to put down these haughty rakshasas.

Ravana, in his underground palace, was awake at all hours hatching plans to obliterate Rama and his army once and for all. He didn't eat, he took to drugs that kept him awake all hours and would swing from being extremely polite to his attendants one minute, to pronouncing death sentences an hour later. He constantly conjured up complicated mechanisms to bring about death to all his enemies.

The next day, Ravana grew desperate. He thought if he could change Sita's mind, that fixture of Rama in her heart, that would be the final solution. He would get the rakshasa attending on her to slip vile potions into her food. But the one rakshasa who was in charge of offering Sita food had grown to like her and would throw the potions away. Each day, just sitting by and listening to Sita's breathing, her sighs, her constant repetition of 'Rama' seemed to fill the rakshasa's mind with peace. She became very loyal to Sita.

The morning of the first day of battle arrived. Ravana listened to his reporters from his underground palace. Conch shells were blown announcing the first declaration of battle from the armies on the bridge. The envoys' experience of the catapult proved useful. With some refinement, the monkey and bear armies had created multiple catapults so that the monkey soldiers could be safely launched onto the inner courtyard of the fort. This avoided the ghastly scaling of the Lanka fort wall; a technique that entailed the defensive rakshasa pouring hot oil on the advancing army and then setting the monkey fur alight.

But once inside the first courtyard of Lanka, there were hills that descended into a valley. Ravana's son released a weapon that spat out a million snakes with venomous poison. Although this poison was to stun the armies, Rama and Lakshmana were also affected.

Ravana took this opportunity to rush to Sita's cell and tell her to come and view the battle scene. She was summoned into the aerial chariot, and from the air, she saw what Ravana told her. 'See! How weak all his attempts are. Down there he lies dead with his brother and all those comical monkeys!' Sita did not see this, as she had fainted from the stench of the poisonous fumes. Ravana was confused. Had the fumes killed her as well, or had her heart stopped beating when Rama's did?

That night, when Ravana learned that Hanuman had recovered much earlier than the others and had found the strength to find out what antidote should be used, he realized he was dealing with a different kind of being. Hanuman had heard that the *Sanjivini* herb was the antidote for the stun drug weapon that Ravana's son had released. But he had no idea what it looked like. So instead of wasting his time, he decided to carry the whole hill with the herb to the chief medical agent of the armies to administer it first to Rama and Lakshmana and then to the rest of the casualties. It worked, and they all awoke refreshed as if from a deep sleep.

Sita had become physically weak, and Ravana had watched how, with the preparation for this war, she had almost stopped eating. He sent one of his rakshasas to place a life-like copy of Rama's decapitated head in a basket beside her. Such gory tricks became commonplace, and Sita could not distinguish between waking and sleep, the horror of a nightmare and the reality of war and what it did to desperate minds. Now, even more than Rama the person, the man she loved, the husband she married, she clung to the name 'Rama' as the anchor to her life, her past, something generated by her own breath, that occupied her mind and heart.

Several days passed on the battlefields at Lanka. Vultures and buzzards were commonplace, picking out the eyes and flesh of the dying. The smell of death pervaded the air and the cries of injured rakshasas, monkeys and bears were a cacophony that sounded like the doomsday end of the planet.

Jambuvan, Sugriva, Lakshmana, Hanuman and Rama fought each day at the battle, rising at daybreak and stopping only at sundown. Rama would visit the camps each night to ensure the remaining soldiers of his armies were at least high in morale and were receiving whatever medicine was available with the utmost care.

Ravana, however, did not condescend to fight in this war against Rama. He felt Rama was too young and inexperienced. Each day he heard how his commanders were falling like pins against the fierce warriors of Rama's armies. Then came the day when he received the news of his son's death. His heart had reached a breaking point. He decided the next day he would show Rama what mettle he was made of.

He woke early and decided that that day Rama would fall and he would have Sita. He told Mandodari, 'Start your prayers. Today you will either be a widow or receive Sita as my wife.' She clicked the last lock on his armour as he strode into his chariot, his silken sashes fluttering like a vulture's wings in high wind.

It was the fourteenth day of the battle. He told his driver to park his chariot within range of where Rama was perched. Rama shot his arrows at Ravana, but each time he could see the arrows bouncing off his chest. He could hear Ravana's thundering laughter mocking him. He did not think of anything else, but that he must put an end to this cause of a meaningless loss of life. He saw Ravana's ten heads. He shot at a head. It fell to the ground. Then another head grew where the previous one had been felled. And so, on and on it went. Ravana's laughter jeered, echoed and shook the very battlefield. Rama was deafened by it to all the other sounds on the field.

Rama had saved the Brahma Astra—a special weapon that he had been warned to use only when all other alternatives had been tried. Rama suddenly saw the secret that kept Ravana. It was his delusions. These multiplied, deceiving him of the truth. That is why the heads, the repeated laughter. Rama focused just as he had when he was at Sita's *swayamvara*; on lifting that bow. All he needed was clarity of purpose; the light of the truth, single-mindedness. 'Let it be only for the good of the world,' he whispered, 'not I, but only good must prevail, whatever else happens.' Rama released the Brahma Astra. A silver arrow

as clear as a laser. It did not whizz through the air with
speed. It flew lightly, forming an arc as it moved silently
across the space between Rama and Ravana. Ravana saw
it coming and recalled Sita's face—the way she looked
when he tried to deceive her in the guise of Rama. He had
nothing left to lose. He shed his cloak, and thrusting his
chest towards the silver arrow was struck by it. He fell to
the ground. Rama was the last face he saw above his head,
kneeling over him. Rama closed the lids of Ravana's dead
eyes. The war to end all wars, between Rama and Ravana,
had ended.

There was such a clanging and hammering of bones,
wood, metal and thudding bodies all around Rama. He just
didn't seem to notice any of this as he knelt down to take a
full look at his opponent lying dead on the ground.

When the armies noticed that Rama was not at his perch,
for one moment they felt all was lost. The rakshasa army
still saw Ravana's chariot. Suddenly a monkey leapt and cut
down its flag. Now they knew, their beloved emperor was
dead and they turned and ran. Vibhishana came forward and
held his brother's head in his lap. He wept. Rama was in
deep sympathy for the predicament. 'That I should call you
in one breath as my friend and give you refuge, and in the
very next should slay your kin down . . .'

Vibhishana replied: 'It must be the simple price of
truth. However bitter these tears are now, I know I will
build my brother's dream of Lanka for it to live longer,
with the beauty of justice.' Rama realized what an amazing
spirit Vibhishana possessed. Once the ceasefire was

declared, Rama said: 'Vibhishana, let us cremate Ravana and celebrate his life for all that he achieved. Let us also be reminded of what happens when our character succumbs to the pride of our achievements. You will now be proclaimed and installed as the king of Lanka.'

Rama was war-weary. He waited till Vibhishana called out to the rakshasas to bring the royal flag that Ravana would be enshrouded in. Announcements were ringing around Lanka: 'Ravana, our Emperor is dead! We are doomed!' That sent panic through the streets, as the rakshasas had never been captured or enslaved before. Also, they felt they had lost the ability of creating illusions and shifting shape after Ravana had died. How would they choose to live or die? That was the haranguing question. Mandodari received the news, partly happy that now Ravana was safe from harming himself, and also that Sita would return to where her heart belonged.

Mandodari's maids-in-waiting were preparing for a cremation pyre for the royal household. The custom was that once a ruler was slain, the victor would take on the wives of the deceased as a mark of victory. Many women who did not want to be enslaved would resort to immolating themselves. The maids were surprised to see Mandodari smiling and waving them aside. 'I'll tell you when I feel like it. But for now, I would like to see this Rama, who without anything has everything.'

Hanuman left Rama, who took to consoling the injured within his reach. He could see how Rama grieved at the death and suffering of the war, and how he felt responsible.

Hanuman was possibly also the only one who knew where Sita could be found. He was in a hurry to reach her and be the first to give her the news of Rama's victory, in case any rakshasa decided to be particularly vindictive and attack her at the news of Ravana's death.

19

Fireproof

It was dark, and Hanuman tried not to be seen on his way to Ashokavan. The entire city was in a worse chaos than when he had leapt around it. Heads, limbs and his foot squelched on mud, water and blood. At last, he saw Sita looking through the bars of her cell. Her eyes did not flicker, only her hand clung to the bar. He came closer. She was barely alive. 'Mother, get dressed. His Lordship is here.'

That was enough. Her heavy heart lightened. She stood. Hanuman bowed to take her blessings. With his head bowed, he said, 'It is customary to receive one's husband with the signs of victory.'

Sita had blessed him and walked on before he could finish instructing her about the ritual bath and wearing fresh clothes and jewellery.

Sita wandered out of her year-long captivity like a lame bird. She stumbled on things in the dark. She always imagined a path out of here, but she did not know the way. She could not make sense of so many dead bodies or that the agonizing cries of the living were all due to her.

Who was she? She started asking herself questions in the third person, like she no longer belonged within her body. Her reply came: She was an orphan. Found by King Janaka, she grew up to be a princess, and then married a man she loved and ever since then, was always in exile, from her parent's home, her married home. In the forests, she had made her home, then was made a captive and taken to Lanka. What was she here for in the first place? It all came back. 'It was that day when I asked for the golden deer. I was tired of it all. I snapped. And that was it? Is this the way it is seen fit to be punished? Just because I'm a woman? Watch all this and be told it is "because of you". I had nothing to do with any of this. I am innocent. And innocence is my blame.'

She came to the bridge that separated Ashokavan from the palace gardens. Now there were flaming torches held aloft by runners to assist the stretcher-bearers. She walked on. Then she saw him. He looked at her, but he could not see her, only beyond her. Then his gaze engaged with hers. She wanted to touch his cheek, feel his palm on her hand when she held his face and uttered his name 'Rama'. But his eyes were like stones, his face a mask. They were standing the length of a sleeping man apart. The monkey and bear soldiers who had fought so valiantly in the name of rescuing Sita now began to shuffle and assemble like extended shadows behind Rama. She stood there dishevelled, yet stately. They felt for her because she too had suffered like them.

Sita, at first, couldn't recognize the voice that was giving an instruction. 'Let it be announced that Lanka is now free. We have not come to conquer this great kingdom. We look upon Vibhishana as the rightful ruler.

'Sita you are also now free from captivity. We have endured much in this war to free you, and all like you, from terror. As you have lived away from us for more than a year, you are free to go wherever you choose.'

'Go', 'Choose', were these his only words of welcome? This was not the Rama she knew. But he *must* be. Was this war fatigue that was making him talk like an automaton?

'If you choose to return with us, now that you have lived apart from us for thirteen months, you must prove to us you are pure.'

'How?' Sita asked enraged.

'Lakshmana!' Rama beckoned.

Sita saw the flint in Lakshmana's hands. His eyes were wet because he had been crying. He hated what he was doing to his beloved sister-in-law and to his beloved brother. Sita had to prove that she was 'pure' by walking through a ring of fire. If she burned, then she would be considered 'impure'. Was there a choice?

'Strike!' Sita commanded. The fire in her spirit lashed out.

Lakshmana struck, heaving for breath as he cried. A small blade of flame emerged from the flint on the ground.

Out of it burst Agni, the God of Fire. 'Rama, what is the need of this proof of her purity? Sita is fireproofed from everything that exists on this earth. Pure? You want to know if she is? How can you measure her every breath? Her very heartbeat has only known two syllables all the time she has spent here. You touch the very walls of her prison, and your fingertips will feel the vibrations of "Ra—ma". Every tree, branch, leaf and petal in Ashokavan only knows the rhythm of her steps to be "ra-ma".' Then Agni grew into a large flame and folding around Sita, guided her to Rama. When he looked at her, his eyes burned with stinging tears as he whispered to her 'Only for their sake Sita'. His repetitions of those words were drowned by the cheers of the assembled bears and monkeys, and even some of the rakshasa clan.

Sita wondered how her life was like a tiny boat tossed by the unpredictable winds of man-made laws. But she had found her voice. Nobody could take that living breath away from her.

20

Deepavali

Lighting the World

When they were alone, Rama could not stop his flood of words. Sita watched him and listened. All his emptiness when she had left, the constant battle to find her, the alliances with Sugriva and Hanuman and the sense of being forsaken by the very gods he worshipped had become a hard rock within him.

By telling Sita about that time, the memory that shaped his thoughts chipped, crumbled and flowed like soft soil with the swiftness of words. Sita threaded it into a garland of stories that she would tell someone in another time in her life.

After a long while, he stopped talking. Only then he looked at Sita and said, 'And you?'

She rose steadily from where she was sitting on the ground in the ruins of what might have once been a merchant's home. Walking up to him, she took his face in both her hands and made him look at her, into her eyes, and beyond her. Her love was too much to bear. He closed his eyes and the tears of longing and understanding flowed.

She pressed her lips on his closed lids and then said, 'Tell me, Rama, what's in a name?'

He could feel in his heart the truth of her waiting with no other thought or feeling, but for him. Rama was his name, but she loved the quality within him when they first set eyes on each other. His strength to love the truth. That was the light she worshipped in him as a man, as her husband. That was Rama, and she reminded him of his true self.

Thirteen long years had passed since their exile had begun. Thirteen dark months had passed from the time Sita was abducted. Neither of them knew of the dark spell that had been cast by Ravana stealing the pot of milk and blood from the holy man or Mandodari's drinking it. But it had set off a chain of dark, unrevealed mysteries of human nature that cast its interminable shadow on Rama and Sita's lives.

The moon was also in its dark cycle. Slowly, through the smoke and the mist and waking tiredness of the city that had been ravaged by war for fourteen days, Rama and Sita felt their companionship returning.

Their bodies entwined against the ruins and dissolved into the arch of eternal lovers.

In the brazen light of day, all damages were accounted for and by Vibhishana's instruction, a mass cremation was held. He reformed the council and with the swift skills of rakshasa town planning, the city and kingdom of Lanka was to be a glittering jewel by the sea. Rama recommended that Vibhishana be installed on the throne, and so, preparations began in fervour. Everyone wanted a celebration—monkeys, bears, rakshasas alike.

Rama, Sita and Lakshmana were central to the rituals performed on the day of Vibhishana's coronation.

Even the rakshasas admitted there was a rhythm to life that they had not known before. Just when Rama, Sita and Lakshmana were sitting watching the jubilant crowds from their apartment, Hanuman came with an urgent message. 'It's from Prince Bharatha.' Rama read out aloud from the palm leaf: 'The end of the fourteenth year fast approaches with the next new moon. I have obeyed your instruction to rule the kingdom during your exile. I have done it in your name. If you do not return to rule this kingdom that has always been your right, I will build a funeral pyre that I will light and step into.'

'We must hurry, otherwise, he will do it,' Rama said, and all three of them leapt up.

It was a long way from Lanka. If they returned to the route Rama's armies came from India, it would take another season and that would be too late. In any case, they hadn't much to carry as they had no possessions. But when the time came to bid farewell to Vibhishana, he piled them with gifts and ships to carry across to Ayodhya. To save

time on their return journey, he escorted Rama, Sita and
Lakshmana with Hanuman, in his aerial chariot across the
ocean. When they landed on the shores of India, Rama and
Sita decided they would like to walk into Ayodhya, just the
way they had left all those many years ago.

It was night by the time they reached the outskirts of
Ayodhya. The new moon was hidden behind the clouds.
In the dwellings of the animal catchers and tamers, one
woman looked out and said: 'Fourteen years have passed.
My child was born when Rama, Sita and Lakshmana left
Ayodhya. Now their exile is over, they promised to return.
But how dark it is, how will they find their way? Hmm . . .
let me see. I have enough oil saved for one lamp. If I light
it and keep it outside our hut, at least they will know they
have reached this bank of the Sarayu.' So, poor as she was,
she drained what little oil she had saved for her dry hair,
fashioned a wick out of cotton and dipped it in oil. She lit
the lamp and kept it outside her hut as she went in.

Another woman was standing out on the balcony of
her house and thought 'Hmm . . . fourteen years of exile
have passed. I hope Rama has not forgotten his promise to
us to bring Sita back safely. Goodness! How dark it is. They
must have travelled miles . . . not even one lamp, as if we
are all in mourning.' Then she caught sight of one solitary
flame at the outskirts of Ayodhya. 'Some poor soul has
thought the same. If all they can afford is one lamp, then
let me lay out at least twenty lamps.' So her servants were
summoned and oil was poured into larger lamps, and they
decided to multiply the lamp count with their own, and on

and on it went as the murmur went around Ayodhya until the entire city was like a night sky full of stars.

Rama and Sita entered a wonderful maze of lit streets, and when Bharatha caught sight of them as he ran down the steps of the palace, the whole city was chiming with celebration with this festival of lights.

After the passing of fourteen years, Rama and Sita were installed at the coronation as king and queen of Ayodhya. Hanuman continued to live in Ayodhya as did Lakshmana, to serve Rama as faithful aides. When storytellers sang of all those years, they always looked towards Valmiki, who inspired them about how the light of human hope saved the world. Finally, the only choice left to us is a path that has great moments of cacophonous dark out of which we make harmonies and light.

21

Never Ending

It's all very well to end a story where we are led to believe it was 'happily ever after'. But all lives have secrets, and all lives like an official version to be told. Also, all lives like to leave behind a note that the secret of life is the search for happiness in light.

After the coronation, Rama and Sita took to having regular audiences with people. Having travelled, and met diverse sects, castes and people of different belief systems they took a genuine interest in how everyone's welfare could be taken care of.

Hanuman and Lakshmana also wandered among people and sought their opinions on a more meaningful way of life. Bharatha's humility in always addressing the matters of state in a council that was to be responsible to Rama when he returned was good planning. People took local governance with seriousness rather than blaming others for things that did not work.

Rama grew more conscious of his role as Head of State. He missed not having his father and mother and their goodwill and advice. Although now that he and Sita were together, there were also different ceremonies and rites that had to be performed as part of their public profile. Strangely, even though they may have been together in the same room, they also were kept apart by matters of State.

The last time they had been together as lovers was the night after the war. In a few months, Sita was glowing. It was announced that the queen was with child. For those who were in their youth when Rama and Sita married, this was the dawning of a new era. For those who had been of Dasaratha's age looked upon this news as awaiting their own grandchild. But what was different from the usual celebrations of weddings and coronations, was that the celebration of awaiting the birth of a child was like a joyful secret that would be revealed in time. There are many reasons; one of them is learning to be patient about the development of life from a cell into a human being and the spiritual evolution from a past life to the new one.

Rama and Sita spent time together and one evening, while they were walking in the gardens as the sun was setting, she said to him: 'Before I have the child, I would love to visit some of the friends we made in the forest. Will you come with me?'

'That would be a good idea! Much as I will miss you even for the few hours you are away, I must let you go alone, as there is a particular situation I must deal with. Return, and I will not let you out of my sight . . .' replied

Rama. They laughed at the thought of being out of each other's sight even for one moment.

Rama tenderly took Sita back to her apartment. Sita was going to cook a special dish for him that evening. 'Don't be too long, will you?'

'How can I when there is a surprise waiting for me?' he said affectionately. Sita laughed holding her full belly, and he saw the woman he loved carrying his child, shuffle happily into the kitchen.

Rama would often go to the pond at dusk and watch the way the light played on the water. The sun's light had gone from the sky, and it was grey and the world reflected in the pond was black and white. As he was taking it in, suddenly he heard a scuffle behind him. He withdrew and stood behind the Neem tree where he would not be seen. An older man was pleading with a younger man: 'How could you send your wife all alone in the night crying, to our home like that! Please have some pity.'

The younger retorted. 'Well . . . if your daughter could find her way in the night to your house without being escorted, who knows where else she goes with such confidence!'

'But please, she is going to have your child. Have some pity!'

Rama was just about to step forward and counsel both men and bring to their attention that the woman bearing a child was more important than their positions as father-in-law and son-in-law in an argument.

'Pity! Your daughter needs to be treated like the wet clothes we beat on the stone to get clean. How dare she become so independent and walk out on her own like that! I'm not like Rama. What a strange man. His wife was thirteen months in the 'care' of Ravana, now she's having a child, and how do we know whose it is!'

Rama felt sick. A whole world turned and changed all that was certain in the past, as the two washermen left, possibly to an arrack shop to drown their differences for a while.

A week passed. Sita was busying herself with gifts for her friends in the forest. Lakshmana was waiting to escort her on the journey.

Everyone cheerily waved and she waved in return saying. 'I'll be back. Get ready to listen to the stories!'

The chariot and its white horses rode steadily out of Ayodhya and Sita kept pointing out to Lakshmana the milestones of their first journey out of the city.

The first stop was at Valmiki's hermitage. It was the farthest from the city, deep in the forest. Lakshmana helped Sita down and then handed her a message. His eyes would not meet hers. She read it and looked up dazed. She barely found the breath to repeat what Rama had written in the message. 'Our citizens doubt the child is mine. It upsets the moral and social order . . .' Is this all he can say and do to OUR child?! Leave me here Lakshmana. Just leave me and go!' Once again, he heard 'Go!' Her rage was engulfing everything like a forest on fire. Lakshmana was so angry with Rama and sick with himself. He rode out of

the forest faster than the speed of wind. He had no thought
of anything else, and when he came to the gorge that had to
be crossed on the way back to Ayodhya, he threw himself
down its treacherous track.

Sita sat a long while with her hands clasping her belly.
Her heart was empty. Her memory was dry. The forest was
still. She kept repeating. 'Is that all he could think? About
what others would say?' After a longer while she decided.
'The earth is my mother. Rama's child and mine will be
born in this forest.'

In the late afternoon, as this was a hermitage, Valmiki
now grown old but still with merry and wise eyes returned
from his day's meditation. He saw Sita. As the Storyteller
of the epic Ramayana, he asked her what happened. When
he heard, he asked her to stay in the hermitage for as long
as she wanted.

It was the month when a new season began to show
itself in the mating of birds, the thawing and rush of water
in the forest spring, and the warming of the earth. Sita
gave birth to a son. She looked at him with mixed feelings
of joy, and loneliness. She had carried him for so long,
now he was a part of her, and yet he was another part. She
named him Lava.

Lava was a demanding infant like any newborn can
be. Sita, of course, did not have any assistants or her own
people to help. Valmiki would help with some of the
fetching of the water from the spring, but Sita did the
cooking, washing and caring.

One day as Lava had grown to be too heavy and had
fallen asleep after a vigorous game of hide and seek, Sita

said to Valmiki, 'I hope you don't mind. I need to get to the spring and wash. Lava's asleep. I didn't want to disturb him, and he certainly won't disturb you.' Valmiki saw absolutely no harm in looking over the sleeping child. Sita left with her bundle of clothes, a few terracotta pots and wooden ladles to wash. Lava was sound asleep. Valmiki let out a great big sigh and thought, 'Why not I meditate here in this very spot instead of going to another place!' So, he closed his eyes and was absorbed in meditation. He entered the heart of his imagination where shining lotuses were floating on sun-dusted water. He found such happiness and peace that he forgot his surroundings. It might have been a short while or a long one, it is not certain, because time had lost all meaning in the space of his imagination. He opened his eyes, and there where Lava should have been sleeping, there was nothing!

'What!' exclaimed Valmiki. 'How could a sleeping baby wander off by itself?' He looked everywhere in the clearing. Under the tulasi shrub, the jasmines, the sides of the hut. 'Where had I been? Has some wild animal taken the baby away? Surely, he would have cried?' he kept asking himself. Then he concluded, 'We hermits can't be trusted to do one practical task!'

In the distance, he could hear Sita singing. It meant she would return in a short while to cook the evening meal. What would he tell her? Valmiki knew Sita's story. She had lost everything, and now as light and joy were returning again into her life, how could he tell her about Lava's disappearance? She trusted him. He was the Storyteller. He had the vision and imagination. What did he do? He plucked a blade of Kusa grass that grew in abundance around the hermitage. He uttered a mantra, and there, in the space where Lava was, another baby replaced him.

Sita called out as she approached the dwelling and Valmiki saw her with Lava on one hip, chattering on about how he seemed to have wandered on to her path. Suddenly, she caught sight of the other baby who now woke and was hungry. She looked puzzled, and Valmiki had to tell her the story of how that happened. 'But where will he go? We can't send him back. He is Lava's brother. Let's name him Kusa.'

Lava and Kusa were inseparable brothers and great companions to their mother. They helped around with the tasks of the others who came and stayed at Valmiki's hermitage. Valmiki, in turn, taught them to sing in verse. Sita would tell them the story of their ancestors and that of their father, Rama.

In Ayodhya, people lived with order and did not lack anything. But they had noticed the day Sita left, joy had left the hearts of all households. Even the washermen commented on it. When Lakshmana did not return, Rama knew this was his final punishment for banishing Sita. Loneliness clung to him like a caged bird with no desire left to fly.

One day, the call to proclaim him King of Kings was made. The Aswamedha was in preparation and a white horse was set free to roam across kingdoms and forests.

The white horse entered a forest farthest away. The reporters and messengers rushed to Rama and said the horse had been seized. This meant that Rama's title of

'King of Kings' was being contested. He rode with his army from Ayodhya and reached the forest when it was dark. He called out, 'On what grounds do you contest this Aswamedha? Show yourself.' Two young men came forward holding the horse. 'Will you really take me and my army on?' asked Rama, amused and surprised. 'Tell me your lineage.' The two young men bowed their heads before they began singing in verse the story of their father and their mother narrated as the Ramayana.

Rama stood a long while listening to the arc of the story, its notes of music shivering with the moonlight on the leaves of overhanging branches. He relived the adventures of his life but with the music of their expression, he gained a deeper understanding of his actions. He ached for Sita. When they finished, Rama asked, 'Where is your mother?'

Sita emerged from behind a tree. Rama came down from his horse and held out his hand. 'Will you return with me and our sons?'

Sita smiled, lighting up the forest. Rama felt his heart sour. She looked at the earth beneath her, it opened into a furrow and Sita turned away, leaving a steady flame of light behind.

Acknowledgements

I thank Gurveen Chaddha, Penguin Random House India, for taking on *The Living Legend* and for being a part of it throughout. To Anushree Kaushal for the best review a writer could hope for in the first reading of a manuscript. To Manali Das for her insightful editing and consideration.

I am indebted to Allarmel Mangathai Calpakkam Karunanidhi Naidu—Ammama—for regaling me with stories from the Ramayana, especially during Deepavali, and my mother, Jayarukmini Naidu, who kept the tradition alive wherever we travelled and lived.

Thanks to all the Ramayanas introduced to me by performance storytellers of Ramlila in Delhi, and temples and koothu in Tamil Nadu and Karnataka. The Sutradhar Storytellers' familiarity with characters—divine, human and demonic—comes from their deep conviction of 'knowing' all the worlds that reside in ourselves.

Immense gratitude to the Royal Literary Fund
Fellowship for providing financial support to me as a writer
in very critical times. *The Living Legend* emerged from an
oral tradition performance work. Writing this made me
engage in further research from Southeast Asia.

For understanding diverse audiences and readerships
thanks are due to Ramanand Sagar's Ramayana and Nima
Poovaya-Smith, the curator of the Ramayana and the
Mewar collection exhibition, for inviting me to narrate the
Ramayana in English to a select audience. Jane Patterson
for building language bridges through storytelling of
the Ramayana in schools in Ilkley, Bradford and West
Yorkshire. To schoolchildren across London for their
feedback on the chapters.

Kath Hamilton of Leicester Haymarket Theatre for
commissioning the production of the Ramayana and its tour.
Thanks to the Arts Council England in the regions of South
East and London for funding the Vayu Naidu Intercultural
Storytelling Theatre to tour internationally to arts venues
in Sweden and Denmark and at the Edinburgh Festival
Fringe. To Isobel Hawson and the Arts Council England
for encouraging storytelling as performance in the theatre.

Thanks to DRUM, an arts initiative in the West
Midlands and in partnership with Her Majesty's Prison
Service at Evesham, for welcoming Ramayana tales. The
workshops that were organized for the inmates was about
listening and transformation.

I am grateful to Prashant Nayak of Milapfest for
programming the Ramayana, with Pandit Shiv Kumar

Sharma and Zakir Hussain in Liverpool and Salford Quays, during Diwali. To Piali Ray, director, Sampad, a Birmingham-based national agency for the development of South Asian arts, for inviting me to speak on panel discussions on the variations in the folk and classical versions of the Ramayana.

Thanks to Ben Haggarty, founder of the Crick Crack Club, a UK-based performance storytelling promoter, for programming the Ramayana across literature and arts festivals as spoken literature across England, Scotland and Wales. To my all-time students and distinguished storytellers Craig Jenkins and Emily Parrish Hennessy for travelling with the Ramayana and me from the Kentish coast to the hills of Edinburgh.

To Mahatma Gandhi, always.

To Imran Sujaat Ali Khan for the Ramayana Project in Pune. Thanks to scholars and workshop leaders of local and regional dimensions that brought the characters to life. Thanks to my sister Viji Vasudev for her mesmerizing productions of the Ramayana at primary schools in Delhi.

Chris Banfield, beloved husband, legend and light-bearer ever, who wanted to hear the entire story in fifteen minutes and so began my future as a storyteller with the Ramayana. Thank you for knowing what is essential in the epic and the production as dramaturg and director at Leicester Haymarket Theatre and its 2001 shows. Music by Colin Seddon has been cosmic. Set and lighting design by Jenny Campbell immortal. My father Aban and mother Jaya for the desk, the house, the food, the love.

For Diana, my well-wisher and faithful mother-in-law,
who drove me on many journeys while performing across
Norfolk. My brothers Hari and Upa, the noblest. My
nephews and nieces from Naidu-Vasudev-Banfield clans:
Keshav, Shibani, Nihaal, Vivek, Santosh, William and
Jae , and additions Anika, Aarav and Myra who hold the
mirror to life.

To Francesca Orsini for reviving interest in local
literatures at SOAS. To Richard Williams for supporting
music and storytelling. To Alka Bagri for her genuine
love of storytelling and the Bagri Foundation, the British
Library and its archives for enhancing the knowledge of
the Ramayana at the Knowledge Centre. The Barbican and
a tube strike that brought an audience of 1400 to attend the
performance in 2010.

Dr Prema Padmanabhan, medical and research
director, ophthalmology, Sankar Nethralaya, Chennai,
for her discerning discussion on the organ of sight, and
perceptions about epics for younger readers. Mala Rao for
her constancy and wisdom in epic matters. For Dr Bhanu
Sivakumar, Dr Priya and Kai, medical practitioners who
revel in the epics and folk stories. Rahul Ramakrishnan for
his reading and fine observations as a reader. To Arundhati
Menon, who has been encouraging us to tell stories to
young children. To Lalita, Sheila, Terry and Bev, my far-
flung family, for their support.

The British Museum and Dr Richard Blurton. Dineke
Koerts for programming the Ramayana at the Tropen
Institute, at the Nethelands. To Girish Karnad for his

early suggestions on the nuances of the performance narrative, to Dr Paula Richman for many discussions on the Ramayanas, and to A.K. Ramanujan, who opened the universe for us to look deeper at perspectives of all the Ramayanas, great and small.

To Rukhsana Ahmad, mentor and friend, for sharing our concerns as writers across continents, and Usha Aroor for inspiring writers with the nuances of characters in the epics.

To Mukulika Banerjee for listening to the Ramayana and for sharing many perspectives on it.

To Davy Nougarede of West End Media Ltd for giving astute advice and seeing spoken and written word evolve. To Jessica Purdue for her time and suggestions. To Ashwati Franklin for sending me exquisite images from the Ramayana collections. To Alice Barron, violinist, who plays the deep, dark green of the forests of England and India, in our performances. To my students at Eton College, UK, for listening and reflecting on differences in the idea of the heroic in the Ramayana and the Odyssey.

To Caryn Solomon and Allen Zimbler for their resolve in valuing the Bushmen's oral traditions thriving in Africa and knowing what it means to keep epic literature alive.

To Namita Gokhale for creating platforms for Sita and a rejuvenation of India's literatures and understanding why writing for young readers is so important.

My eternal gratitude to Swami Bhuteshananda, Swami Dayatmananda, Swami Sarvasthananda, Swami Tripurananda, Swami Bhuvanatmananda and the dedicated

monks of the Ramakrishna Order, who constantly open
the deeper foundational philosophy and practice of the
significance of this epic.

What love or desire or grace made me write this, to
that, an evergrowing forest of thanks.

Scan QR code to access the
Penguin Random House India website